Dana Hammer
My Best Friend Athena

Published by: Cinnabar Moth Publishing LLC
Santa Fe, New Mexico

Cover Design by: Ira Geneve

ISBN-13: 978-1-953971-63-0
Library of Congress Control Number: 2022947033

My Best Friend Athena

DANA HAMMER

CHAPTER ONE

Normally, when I arrive at school, I'm tired and cold and grumpy, but not today! Because today I've got the World's Coolest Necklace, and everyone's gonna notice it and give me compliments. It's a "statement" necklace, and I got it at an old lady's estate sale yesterday. I was shopping with my best friend, Athena, when I saw it.

It was sitting on a dresser, with a bunch of other jewelry, but this necklace was the only one that caught my eye. It's a large octopus, with jewel-covered tentacles, and two pearls for eyes. I tried it on, and it looked like the tentacles were reaching around my neck, trying to choke me.

I'd never seen anything so cool in my life. It was $20, which was more than I had, but luckily Athena was there, and she bought it for me. Athena always has lots of money, because she's a rich kid, but that's NOT why I'm friends with her.

Anyway, she saw how sad I was that I couldn't afford the necklace and she just bought it for me, probably because she has excellent taste and could see what a great investment it would be. She said it was "quirky" and "an interesting piece," which I happen to know is code for "high fashion."

My mom said it was "tacky garbage" but she doesn't know about fashion. She mostly wears gym clothes, even when she's not at the gym, and she never wears jewelry, except her wedding ring.

Anyway, I stride into the hall at school, in a great mood. I'm shivering because I refuse to wear a coat to cover up my necklace, but it's totally worth it. I wave at people I'd never normally wave at, and smile a lot, kind of pushing my neck and chest out to make the necklace more noticeable. I worry that the lights aren't shining on it properly. I really want people to see the shiny pearls it has for eyes.

Everyone is milling around in the hall, like they always do before school starts. I stand in front of my locker, waiting for my friends to see me and say, "OH MY GOD THAT'S THE COOLEST NECKLACE, WHERE DID YOU GET IT?" And then I'll say, "Why it's vintage, of course," and then I'll be "The Girl With the Vintage Statement Necklace," not just "Athena's Friend Who's

Good at Math." Actually, I'll be "Athena's Friend Who Has Exquisite Taste in Necklaces and is Also Good at Math."

Yeah! That's who I'll be!

The new kid, Daniel, is staring at me. I don't know Daniel very well. He has brown hair, and he wears sweatpants almost every day—that's all I know. But I'm always nice to new kids—it's my policy. It's actually a really good policy, because this one time, there was a new kid at school, and we all thought she was kind of weird, because she had ratty hair and made weird jokes, and was always showing us pictures of her bird, which was not like, a pet bird, but a crow. No one wanted to be friends with her, but then, after she moved, we found out she was actually the daughter of a famous actress who was here filming a role. We could have been hanging out at that famous actress's house that WHOLE TIME.

Anyway, my point is, it's always a good idea to be nice to new kids, so I smile at Daniel, to be friendly.

He doesn't smile back. Instead he says, "Why are you pushing your chest out like that?"

Immediately, I'm sorry I smiled at him. This boy is rude and tacky.

"I'm not," I snap, crossing my arms over my chest, hunching over a little.

"Are you trying to make your boobs look bigger?"

He has a smirk on his face, and I want to die. Is that what everyone's been thinking all morning? That I'm just trying to draw attention to my boobs? Is everyone talking about it? Has anyone even noticed my necklace?

I remember last month when a tissue fell out of Fiona Lieberman's pocket, and Toya picked it up and said that Fiona had been stuffing her bra with it, and everyone totally believed Toya, even though I SAW the tissue fall out of her pocket, NOT her bra, and I told everyone that. But people would rather make fun of Fiona than believe the truth, because the truth—that a tissue fell out of a pocket—is not a very good story at all.

Now people will make fun of me, just like they made fun of Fiona, and together we'll be "The Girls Who Try to Make Their Boobs Look Bigger."

My face gets hot, and I try to think of something clever to say, but then Daniel is standing right in front of me. His eyes are small and beady, and he reaches out for my necklace.

"Wow, cool necklace!"

And just like that, I'm cheered up. "Thank you!"

He pulls the octopus toward him, examining the pearl eyes, and I feel a rush of relief. See, this is the reason it's good to wear interesting stuff. Now, instead of an awkward conversation about my chest, we're having a nice, polite, interaction. He was being a jerk, and now he's being a perfect gentleman. That's the power of jewelry.

A weird smirk crosses his face. He looks at me in the eyes, and then, all of a sudden—he gives the necklace a hard yank.

"OUCH!" I squeal.

The chain breaks, and the octopus falls to the ground. As soon as it hits, one of the pearls falls out and skitters under my locker, probably never to be seen again. Not until someday in a century or so, when they tear down this school, and some demolition worker finds it and takes it home, laughing about the stupid kid who was stupid enough to lose such a beautiful pearl.

Daniel laughs. He laughs and laughs, and now some people are standing around watching while I try to think what do to. Should I hit him? Should I tell on him? Should I say something witty and mean to make him feel bad?

I do none of those things. Instead I just bend over and pick up the pieces of my necklace. My eyes fill with tears, but I blink them away. It would NOT be good if people saw me crying at school, especially since I used to have a reputation for being kind of a crybaby.

"I'm not a crybaby anymore. I'm a sophisticated young lady who is cool and fun. I will not let myself be bullied." I repeat this in my head a couple of times, then stand, my hands full of broken necklace, ready to face Daniel and give him a piece of my mind. I'm going to stand up for myself. I'm going to make him apologize. I'm going to demand that he replace my necklace with something of equal or greater value.

But Daniel is gone already, and no one is looking at me anymore. Show's over, I guess.

I can't believe that just happened. I'm Fanny! No one bullies me! I'm friends with everyone, including Athena, the most popular girl in school. I'M NICE!

Just then, Athena comes up to me, looking polished and posh, as always. She's got on a dove gray coat that looks expensive. It matches her eyes exactly.

"Fanny! What happened to your necklace?"

I'm still holding the pieces, and I can feel my face crumple.

"You know that new kid, Daniel? He broke it."

"He broke it? How?"

"He just reached out and broke it! On purpose!"

Athena frowns with that look she sometimes gets that makes her seem a lot older than eleven.

"Nevermind him. We can fix it. Let's go to the library. I think Mr. Dale has a jewelry repair kit in his desk."

"Really? That's weird," I say, because it is.

Athena shrugs. "The man likes jewelry. Come on, let's go."

We go to the library, and I'm glad to be there. I love libraries with their old-book smells and comfy bean bag chairs. Our school library is especially cool, because it was built in the 1920s, and everything is very art-deco and fancy. It doesn't match the rest of the school at all.

The librarian, Mr. Dale, really likes us. Well... he likes Athena. Everyone likes Athena. So he doesn't mind helping us out at all when Athena asks him to fix my necklace. He is a very capable, talented man. In addition to being a librarian, which is arguably the best job a person can have, he can fix jewelry, ride a unicycle, and he even plays on a softball league. He's a real Jack of All Trades, we're lucky to have him in this school.

While Mr. Dale fixes my necklace for me, Athena and I roam around the bookshelves, looking for stuff to read. There are a few other kids in the library too. We say hi to them as we pass them. They all smile at Athena, because she's super nice, and everyone wants to be her friend.

They don't feel that way about me. I'm just Fanny, her

much-less-cool best friend. I don't have her gorgeous gray eyes, or her awesome artistic talents. I'm pale, with light hair and eyes, all washed out and colorless, with none of Athena's edgy coolness. I'm just an ordinary girl with a name that means "butt."

I once asked my mom why she gave me such a terrible name.

"Why would you name me Fanny? You named me after a butt!"

She got really mad when I said that.

"You are named after my mother, and you know it. Fanny is a beautiful name, a family name. You should be proud to have it!"

It's easy for my mom to say that, because she's named Linda, which doesn't mean any kind of body part. Nobody named Linda gets made fun of for her name.

I've picked out a mystery book. It's one of those old-fashioned ones where the grownups are useless and the kids are in charge of solving crimes. I love books like that, even if they're not very realistic.

Athena has chosen a book about how to make your own macrame art. Athena is a wonderful artist. She can paint anything she decides to, and she can make lots of fancy crafts, too. Her birthday gifts are always the best, because she makes them herself, and they're always just what you wanted, but didn't know you wanted until she gave it to you.

I'm not good at art. At all. Everything I draw looks like a little kid drew it, with uneven lines and weird proportions. My paintings all look like big blobs of shapeless color. I once managed to slice off the tip of my finger with a paper cutter, when we were doing origami. Who hurts themselves on origami day? People who are really bad at art, that's who.

But there is one thing Athena and I are equally good at, and that's math. In fact, that's how we became friends, in second grade. I had just moved to Athens, Georgia, with my family. I was the new kid and didn't have any friends. I sat next to Athena, and I noticed that we both did our math problems quickly, and we always got 100% on our tests and assignments.

We got bored with the math the other kids were doing, so we started to make our own math worksheets, and we gave them to each other, just for fun. After a while, our teacher found out what we were doing, and she gave us our own little math class, just us two, where we did advanced math together. It was cool to have someone who understood how fun math was, who didn't think it was boring or stupid. She was easily the prettiest girl in our class, and she always had the best clothes, and the best sense of humor.

When you spend a lot of time with another person, especially such a cool person, you just naturally become friends. Soon we were playing together at recess and eating lunch together and sleeping over at each other's houses. We were best friends, and we were inseparable.

Now we are the president and Vice President of the Meadow Ridge Charter School Math Club, otherwise known as The Mathmagicians.

I know how nerdy that sounds, but it's actually pretty cool. We get to go to competitions and tournaments. We even got to go to Washington DC last year, which was fun for everybody, but it was very special for me, because that's where I discovered my secret talent.

As long as I can remember, I've liked to sing, but never in front of people. I've always sung when I was alone, in the shower, while doing the dishes, whenever my parents leave the house. I'll get a hairbrush and pretend it's my microphone and sing to my own choreographed dance moves. I saw a girl doing that in an old movie one time, and decided to try it, and you know what? It's fun.

Anyway, until Washington DC, I'd never, ever sang in front of other people. You see, I have really bad stage fright. Last month, when I had to give my oral report on Helen Keller,

I got so nervous that I started giggling. Once I started giggling, I couldn't stop. I couldn't breathe, much less give my report.

It was so much worse, because I'd spent the whole night before practicing talking in front of a group. I read it in front of my parents, even though I could tell they were bored and didn't really care about Helen Keller. I practiced in front of a mirror. I was wearing my favorite red dress that always makes me feel confident and pretty, and I pulled my hair back into a ponytail so it wouldn't get in my face when I talked. I'd done so much prep-work, and I fell to pieces anyway.

Mrs. Caldwell had to ask me to go into the hall until I could calm myself. It was super embarrassing. I never did give my report, and I got a D on that assignment. Which, personally, I think is totally unfair. I mean, I still DID the report, I just didn't read it in front of the class very well. I should have gotten at least a C. But Mrs. Caldwell said that being able to speak in front of people is an incredibly important life skill, and one we will all probably need in life, at some point.

Athena gave her report on the philosopher Plato, and she never giggled once. She stood in front of the class and talked about a guy most of the kids had never even heard of and made him sound interesting. Everyone watched her like she was a celebrity giving a performance. And she even did extra credit, and brought in a bunch of homemade baklava, and passed it out to everyone. It was delicious.

Of course, she got an A.

My point is, I get nervous in front of people. But this day, in Washington DC, there was a street performer playing her guitar and singing outside the Smithsonian. She had long dread-locks and wore a brightly printed skirt, and no shoes, and she was the coolest thing I'd ever seen. And best of all, the song she was singing, "Life of Ice," happens to be my favorite song, one that I always sing to myself when I'm alone.

So when I heard this lady singing my song, I couldn't help but sing along, quietly, just for myself. But I guess the performer noticed me singing, and how much I was enjoying it, because she stretched out her arm to me, inviting me to sing with her.

I froze. I wanted to sing the song, but all the kids from Math Club were there, watching, and a bunch of other people, too. There were tourists all over the place, and most of them had phones and cameras. I imagined some nice family from Chicago sitting and watching their vacation video, and hearing me sing and saying "Oh, fast forward it. This girl is the worst." My voice got snuffed out in my throat, like a candle. I couldn't breathe right. I felt dizzy.

Then, Athena patted me on the shoulder. She looked me in the eyes and said, "Go. Sing."

And all at once, this rush of bravery and confidence washed over me. I felt like I could sing in front of a thousand people, a million people, and they would all love me. How could they not love me? I was lovable and talented and cool.

I walked right up to the lady and started singing, loud and strong.

And you know what? People did love me. They all clapped and cheered, and later, when Athena showed me the video she took of the performance, I nearly cried. It was that good.

I know it's not nice to brag. I do. But I'm just being honest. I'm a really, really good singer. And someday, I'm gonna be able to sing in front of an audience again. I've tried a few other times, in front of my parents, and once at the school talent show (that was a nightmare), but I've never been able to get my confidence back. Which is disappointing.

But I know one day, it'll happen again. In the meantime, I'll keep practicing.

Oh, there's one other reason I really like to sing, a reason that I feel kind of bad about.

Athena can't sing very well. At all.

14

CHAPTER TWO

After the library, we headed to class, and discovered that today we have a guest. The guest is a lady named Mrs. Harris from the Fancy Ladies Guild. She came once last year, to try to get us interested in cotillion, which kind of made me feel bad for her. I mean, who wants to do cotillion? Nobody, and it showed.

Now she stands in front of us with a big, lipsticky smile on her face, wearing a pink suit. Where does she think she is? Why is she wearing a suit? Maybe she has a job interview after this and doesn't have time to go home and change.

"I'm here today to talk to you young ladies about an exciting opportunity! This year, as fifth graders, you are finally eligible to enter the Junior Miss Super Pretty Pageant!"

She looks around grinning, like she expects us to cheer. When no one does, she blinks once, and continues.

"As a contestant in the pageant, you'll learn poise, confidence, and how to present yourself to the public. Best of all, you'll make friends for life. I met my best friend Mandy at Junior Miss tryouts."

Her smile flickers.

"Of course, that ended badly."

I meet Athena's eyes and give her a "what the heck" look. She shrugs back at me. We smile.

"But we welcome all girls to come to our orientation meeting this Friday at 7pm at the Grange Hall downtown."

"What do we have to do to apply?"

That's Toya. Toya is going to enter the pageant, and she is going to win, I'm sure. She's that kind of girl. Her hair is always in perfect braids, with perfectly placed bows and clips and headbands, and she gets manicures. Like real manicures, at a salon, with real nail polish, not the weird peel-off stuff my mom still gets for me—the kind with kittens and sparkles on the bottle.

Mrs. Harris smiles. She has a shiny smile, like her teeth are covered in Vaseline.

"I'm so glad you asked! You'll need to bring this filled-out permission slip, signed by your parent or legal guardian. Then you'll need to attend the orientation I mentioned, where you'll meet all the other girls, get familiar with the rules of the pageant, and start learning the choreography for the opening dance number."

Toya smiles and nods, looking eager.

"And of course, you'll want to start thinking about what your talent will be. When I was on the circuit, I always did a tap dance routine. But your talent can be whatever you want. Ballet dancing, hip-hop dancing, Irish step dancing, baton twirling, singing... the sky's the limit."

I feel something straighten my spine, and I'm suddenly sitting up taller. Singing? I'd never really thought about entering a pageant before, but Mrs. Harris is right. Singing is a great talent for a pageant. Maybe this could be my shot! Maybe this will help me get over my stage fright.

"And of course, we can't forget the prizes. The winner of the Junior Miss Super Pretty Pageant wins a one-thousand-dollar savings bond, a year-long membership to Fit and Fantastic Girls Fitness Center, a free manicure at Nailed It Nail Salon, and of course, she will be honored at the Annual Founders Day Parade, where she will ride on her very own float!"

One thousand dollars! That's more money than I've ever had. I think of all the things I could spend it on. New shoes. I could buy my own subscription to Netflix, so I could watch whatever I want without the parental controls. I could buy a plane ticket and fly to Hawaii.

Like I said, I've never wanted to be a pageant girl before... but now...

"Does anyone have any questions?"

Mrs. Harris folds her arms in front of her, politely.

Athena raises her hand.

"Yes, young lady?"

Athena cocks her head, and I cringe, because I know that look. Athena's about to give this woman a piece of her mind.

"How do you justify keeping this nonsense tradition alive?"

Mrs. Harris frowns.

"I'm sorry?"

Athena glares. "Shouldn't you be valuing girls for things other than their beauty?"

Mrs. Harris smiles, but this smile is different than her former one. This one is smarter, meaner. Much less shiny.

"I see someone's been talking to a first-year college student." Mrs. Harris smirks. It's super patronizing, and I want to warn her that she shouldn't have given Athena that kind of look. I've seen what happens when people give her that look, and it rarely ends well for them.

"I'll have you know that the Junior Miss Super Pretty

Pageant DOES honor girls for more than their beauty. That's why we have a talent portion. That's why we have a question-and-answer session, where girls can speak their minds on any number of topics."

"And that's why you have a swimsuit competition, too, right?"

Athena crosses her hands over her chest, defiant.

"Athena, that's enough!"

Mrs. Caldwell is standing up behind her desk now, glaring at Athena.

Athena looks down at her desk. She will be quiet now, because she doesn't want to get in trouble, but I can tell that she's furious. Her hands are gripping the sides of her desk like she's trying to keep it from flying away in a tornado.

My stomach sinks. What will happen if I do the pageant? What will Athena think? Will she be mad at me? Will she stop being friends with me?

I take a deep breath. I have to do this pageant. If I ever want to be a professional singer, I need to get over my stage fright, and the sooner the better. This is a great opportunity for me.

And the money doesn't hurt, either.

If Athena can't see that, and if she won't support me,

then she's not that good of a friend.

———————

Athena is at my house for dinner tonight. She eats at our house a lot. She seems to like it better at my house, which doesn't make any sense, because her house is this gigantic mansion with big white columns and spiral staircases.

I love it at her house. It makes me feel like royalty when I get to walk around their gardens, or float in their swimming pool, or sit and watch a movie in their OWN PRIVATE MOVIE THE-ATER, or when their CHEF asks me what I want for dinner, and no matter what I say, she COOKS IT FOR ME.

My house is nothing like that. It's all one story, with three bedrooms. Nothing is fancy or expensive. All our furniture is from Ikea, or it's old stuff that Grandma and Grandpa got rid of before they moved to Arizona. We don't have a chef, like Athe-na does. My mom cooks ordinary things like spaghetti and fish sticks. We have brown carpet instead of polished marble. We have a plastic wading pool, for when it gets really hot.

Why Athena even agrees to set foot in my house is a mystery.

Now she's happily grabbing a slice of pizza from the card-board box that's sitting in the middle of the table. Mom had a rough day at work, and said she was too tired to cook, so we're having pizza. I hate to admit it, but I love it when mom has hard days at work, for just this reason. I especially like this white pizza, with spinach and red pepper flakes. It's gooey and cheesy and perfect.

In between bites, Athena is talking about our day, while my parents listen as if she's telling the greatest story ever.

"So this lady, Mrs. Harris came to our class today, trying to get us girls to enter the Pretty Pretty Princess Pageant or whatever—"

"Junior Miss Super Pretty Pageant," I correct.

"Yeah. That. Anyway, I asked her why she insists on continuing this stupid, sexist tradition, and she didn't like that at all."

My mom slaps the table and laughs. She is delighted with Athena.

"I bet she didn't. You go, girl!"

Sigh. My mom is always saying things like "you go, girl" that probably made sense when she was a kid, but are kind of uncool and weird now. You go girl? Go where? Why? Where is she supposed to go?

My dad smiles at Athena, and I know what he's thinking. He's wishing Athena was his daughter, instead of me. She's spunky and smart. She stands up for what she believes in.

I look at the table. I can feel my face burning hot.

"And to waste class time for something like that. Like, aren't we supposed to be learning?" Athena continues. "It's just ridiculous. Wasn't it ridiculous, Fanny?"

I look up, glancing around at Athena and my parents. I feel a lump in my throat. It would be so easy to just agree with Athena and get on with dinner, and never think about the pageant again.

But something stops me. It's an image. An image of me, on a stage, singing in front of my parents, my friends, the whole town. I'm wearing a bright blue dress covered in sequins, and my hair is in a grown-up chignon. I'm singing like a professional, and it's beautiful.

"Actually," I hear myself say, "I don't think it's all that ridiculous."

Athena blinks.

My mom looks confused, like I just announced that I want to become a sword swallower when I grow up.

Actually, that would be a pretty cool job, but now is not the time to get into that.

"What?" Athena asks, politely.

"I mean..." I nearly drop my slice of pizza, because my hand is shaking. I set the pizza down on my plate. "I mean, you can win some really cool prizes."

Athena scoffs. "A gym membership and a manicure. Who do they think they're kidding?" She puts on a mocking voice. "We care about girls' brains, just don't get too fat, fatties."

"And a thousand dollars!" It makes me mad that she left that out. The thousand dollars is the best part.

Athena frowns at me, looking puzzled. "Fanny... do you want to do the pageant?"

"I don't know. Maybe."

"Oh."

Athena looks uncomfortable now, and a little embarrassed. Why is she embarrassed? I'm the one who wants to do the pageant.

My parents look at each other and at us, seeming unsure what to do. I need to break the tension, so I start babbling, like I do.

"I mean, I'm thinking about it. It might help me to get over my stage fright."

Athena bites her lip. "Well... I mean, do you remember the talent show, Fanny?"

Of course I remember the talent show. I'd practiced for weeks on my song, getting it just right, even adding some dance moves. Not fancy dance moves, like a choreographer would choose, but fun dance moves—the kind you see cool girls doing on TikTok. I had the best outfit too—light oceanic colors with a sequined infinity scarf, and knee-high boots. I looked so cute!

And then, when it was my turn to sing, I couldn't even go onstage. I mean, my legs wouldn't move. It was like a witch froze me in a block of cement or something.

Athena hadn't been there that night; she'd been home sick with the flu. But she'd heard about it from, well, everyone.

It wasn't my finest hour.

"So? That was months ago. I want to try again. I think I can do it this time."

"Well, honey, that's great if you want to do that pageant," says my dad, at the same time my mom says "I don't know honey..."

"Pageants are not really—" Mom starts.

"I mean, as long as it's not too—" Dad says.

My parents look at each other, confused that they're not on the same page. I know this means they're about to start bickering, so I excuse myself and Athena and we go up to my bedroom. My parents don't fight a LOT, but when they do, it's really annoying, because it just goes on and on, with lots of sarcasm and eye rolling. Tedious.

We sit down on the bed in my room, and Athena grabs a pink throw pillow and pulls it onto her lap.

"I'm sorry, Fanny. I didn't know you wanted to do the

pageant. I hope I didn't hurt your feelings or anything."

This makes me feel a lot better. I was afraid she'd be mad or disappointed or something. Nothing is worse than having your best friend be mad at you.

"That's ok," I say. "You didn't know."

"Are you sure though? Are you positive?"

"Yeah, I think so."

Athena nods seriously. "Ok then. I guess we'd better start getting ready. Do you think I could show some of my paintings for the talent portion? Or is that not the kind of talent they want? These things seem very… dance-centered."

"Wait... what? A minute ago you thought the pageant was stupid."

"I still do. But I don't think you're stupid, and if this is what you want to do, then I support it."

I don't like where this is headed.

"But that doesn't mean you have to do it too!"

She laughs. "Don't be silly. I wouldn't let you do this alone. We're best friends. We do things together."

I smile at her, but it's a fake smile. I know she's trying to be supportive. I know she's trying to be nice. I should be really, really happy to have such a great friend.

25

But I can't help but worry... how will anyone notice me, next to her?

CHAPTER THREE

The next day at school, I'm super excited, because Gemma's coming back!

It's before school, and I'm out on the playground area, waiting for Gemma to arrive. Not very many kids are here yet, so there's not as much excitement as there should be. I have to be the welcome home parade, all by myself. I wish the play area was more festive, but it's just a lot of boring old blacktop. I should have showed up earlier to decorate. I should have brought balloons, and maybe cupcakes. Maybe I could have even got the school band to play! But it's too late for that now. Bummer.

And then, there she is! Wheeling past the gate, onto the blacktop. I see her and squeal.

"Gemma!"

I run to meet her and jump into her wheelchair and hug her. She's been in France for the past four months, and I've missed her so much. She looks the same as she did when she left, except her red hair is longer, and less curly. She's also wearing a cute little tailored jacket with bows on it that is so French I want to die.

She hugs me back and wheels us in circles, which I love. The teachers and recess monitors HATE it when she gives me wheelchair rides, probably because they're afraid I'm gonna hurt Gemma somehow, or maybe they're worried that Gemma will lose control and spill me onto the blacktop or something, and the school will have to fork out money for medical bills and lawsuit fees. But they don't need to worry. Gemma and I are expert tandem wheelchair riders. We have lots of practice.

"How was France?" I ask as we circle the playground.

"France was awesome. You know what I got to do while I was there?"

"What?"

Gemma's eyes widen then narrow in that way they do when she's being really intense.

"I ate horse meat."

"WHAT?"

Gemma giggles. "I ate horse meat. It wasn't too bad, but not really my thing."

My stomach squashes. Gross.

"But... you can't eat horses!"

She shrugs. "You can in France. Actually, it makes sense when you think about it. I mean, how is it different to eat a horse than a cow?"

I think of Black Beauty and Flicka and My Little Ponies.

"It just is."

"No it's not. Anyway, I was thinking the next time we go to France, I'll see if my parents will let me taxidermy one."

I stand up, getting out of her chair.

"Are you messing with me?"

"I mean, not a young, healthy pony. But maybe an old sick horse, who's ready to die anyway."

"You're messing with me."

She smiles at me. "Maybe."

I laugh. "Same old Gemma. I've missed your jokes."

But the truth is, I'm not entirely sure if she's kidding or not. She says lots of weird stuff all the time, and usually I just laugh, but at her house, there really are a bunch of taxidermied animals displayed all over the place. Birds, and fish, and a gigantic elk head that stares down at you from over the fireplace with sad, judgmental eyes.

She might kill and stuff a horse.

29

So... I decide to just leave it.

A big rubber ball flies through the air and hits Gemma in the head, knocking her glasses to the ground.

I look around to see where it came from. Some kids are playing kickball on the field, and they lost their ball.

"OW!"

Gemma presses her hand to her face, where she got hit.

One of the kickball players yells "Sorry!"

"Are you ok?" I ask Gemma, kicking the ball back to the kickball players.

"Yeah. Just lost my glasses."

"Oh, right."

But as I lean over to pick them up, Daniel, the new kid, grabs them. I'm still mad at him for the necklace incident, but I still have manners, and I appreciate it when someone helps one of my friends.

"Thanks," I say to him, because I'm obviously a bit slow, and don't realize that he's not trying to be helpful. He's not trying to pick up Gemma's glasses for her. He's being mean, and he just stands there, holding the glasses and grinning.

"Um, can I have my glasses?" Gemma asks. She looks confused, and I don't blame her. What is this kid doing?

"Come get 'em." he smirks, like this is such a cool joke.

I roll my eyes. "Not funny. Give her her glasses back."

"Like I said, come get 'em." He dangles the glasses high overhead.

Gemma says something in French, which I assume is not very complimentary, because her whole face is full of rage when she says it. It sounds scary.

Daniel steps closer, like he's going to hand her the glasses. Gemma extends her hand to take them, but he jumps back at the last minute.

"Dude. Stop being a douche nozzle!" I yell. I have had it with this kid.

Then, Athena is there, hands on her hips, looking like a superhero. All she needs is a cape. "HEY," she shouts at Daniel.

Daniel turns and sees Athena standing there. His face flickers, and he doesn't look so confident anymore. Like most kids (and some grownups), he's intimidated by Athena.

"Gemma is off-limits." She is calm, and very adult-sounding. I wish I could sound like that.

Daniel sticks his lower jaw out in a gross pout. It makes him look like a big baby. "I was just kidding around. It's not like she even knows what I'm saying anyway. She's a retard."

31

It happens so fast I can hardly process it. Athena snatches the glasses from Daniel, tosses them to Gemma, and then swipes his knee with her shiny black boot, sending him sprawling to the ground.

He lands on his back, and the wind is knocked out of him. He gasps for air. He sounds like he might have a heart attack or something.

Athena stands over him and walks around, like a hawk circling its prey. She's so cool and scary, like the hero in an action movie.

Other kids have noticed what's happening, and they gather around, watching. Some of them are cheering, but most of them are just talking excitedly to each other. It's not every day they get to see something like this, and I totally get why they're excited. Still, it's kind of creepy too, how much they seem to enjoy this, when they really don't have any idea what's going on, or why this is happening.

"We don't use that word when talking about people, especially not the lovely Gemma Gardener," Athena says.

Daniel continues to gasp. He doesn't look so good. His face is covered in sweat, and he's all flushed and red.

I wonder if he'll pee his pants. One time, last year, two

boys got in a fight, and one of them got scared and wet himself. He still hasn't lived it down. He will always be "The Boy Who Peed His Pants at School."

Daniel doesn't pee, though. His sweatpants remain dry. He just gasps and pants.

I glance at Gemma. She is quiet, but I can tell she's delighted. Her eyes are all sparkly, and she's sitting on the edge of her seat.

"Do you understand?" Athena asks.

Daniel nods, looking miserable.

"Good."

And before anyone can do anything, Athena kicks him, right in the arm.

By now, the recess monitor is aware of what's happened, and she comes and grabs Athena by the arm.

"What has gotten into you, Athena? To the principal's office! Now!"

Athena grins merrily at Gemma and waves. "Welcome back, Gemma! It's so good to see you again!"

The recess monitor grumbles and leads Athena inside, while the kids all start talking about what just happened.

"Did you see?"

"That was so badass."

"Her first day back—"

"Don't know what he was thinking..."

Daniel pulls himself to his feet and brushes himself off. His face is red. He looks around and moves close to Gemma. He leans down and whispers.

"Retard."

Then he runs away.

————

Athena doesn't come to class when the bell rings, and I guess that's because she's still in the principal's office. I wonder how much trouble she'll be in. Will they suspend her? Will she be expelled? Will the police come and arrest her for assault?

I can't let that happen. Fortunately, I have a plan. I need to get to the principal's office. I'll explain exactly what happened, and hope that it helps Athena. I'm sure if they understand that Athena was defending Gemma, they'll go easy on her.

It's art class, and Gemma is sitting next to me at the art table, chattering away about how crepe paper can be used to make fairly realistic-looking intestines. I can't concentrate on what she's saying though, because I'm too worried about Athena.

"Do you want to come with me to go talk to the principal?" I ask.

Gemma stops talking about blood and guts. "Do you think it'll help?"

"I don't know. But we should try."

Gemma nods, and I'm glad. Our testimony will be much more effective coming from her, since she was the one getting bullied.

I raise my hand to ask to be excused, but as I do so, there's a loud sound in the hallway.

"WHERE IS MY DAUGHTER?"

In the hallway, I see Athena's dad, Mr. Cronusson. He is stomping toward the principal's office, ignoring the hall monitor. He's a huge man with a big round chest, and fierce, intelligent eyes. As always, he wears a suit and tie.

He is, frankly, terrifying. I feel bad for Arty the hall monitor, who tries to stop Mr. Cronusson, because Mr. Cronusson cannot be stopped.

"Sir, you can't just walk in there. You have to have—"

Mr. Cronusson places a hand on Arty's forehead and pushes him away. Poor Arty stumbles and falls on his butt.

Mr. Cronusson doesn't even look at him. He just keeps walking.

I know one thing for certain. I can't miss this.

"Mrs. Caldwell, I need to be excused!"

Mrs. Caldwell frowns at me. "Is there a problem?"

"I got my period!"

The kids around me titter, but I don't care. Like all the puberty pamphlets say, a period is nothing to be ashamed of.

"Well, ok then. Take the hall pass."

"Dude," Gemma whispers, poking me in the side.

Oh right. I was supposed to bring her with me.

"Sorry," I whisper to her.

I snatch the hall pass and exit the room. The hall pass is a gigantic pink laminated dog bone for some reason, and I hate carrying it. Especially because I have no idea if the other kids who touch it have washed their hands after taking it to the bathroom. But this is what I have to do to get out of class, so needs must .

In the hall, Mr. Cronusson is standing outside the principal's office now, arms crossed over his chest. The tailoring on his suit is exquisite, and he looks commanding and powerful.

"ATHENA! I command you to leave that office at once!"

Principal Parrish emerges from the doorway and tries to exert his authority. However, Mr. Parrish is about a foot shorter than Mr. Cronusson, with a soft, weak jaw, a bald head, and a wobbly belly. It is not a fair fight.

"Mr. Cronusson, I understand that you're upset. If you could just come inside and sit down, we can discuss it."

"I am a busy man, and my daughter has done nothing wrong. You will release her from your clutches at once."

"My... clutches?" Mr. Parrish shakes his head, like he's never heard anything like this before. He probably hasn't.

"Yes. You will send her back to class, where she can get on with her studies. My daughter is a warrior in service of courage, justice, and the rule of law. Any man who attempts to hinder her in this noble pursuit is an enemy. Not just an enemy of civilization, but an enemy of me, personally."

Mr. Cronusson glares at Mr. Parrish, as if to say, "your move." It's very cool and intimidating.

Mr. Parrish stares at him for a few moments, glaring. Then he breaks eye contact. His shoulders slump. He is defeated. He turns to the office and yells inside.

"Kenny? Tell Athena she can go back to class."

His voice cracks a little when he yells, and I can tell that Mr. Parrish hates himself. He wishes he were as tough as Mr. Cronusson, and he wishes he didn't give in. But he did, and he knows it, and he's so embarrassed it makes me embarrassed for him. It's hard to watch.

Mr. Cronusson gives a curt nod and spins on his heel, striding away.

I can't help it. I giggle from where I'm hiding. I can see where Athena gets her fierceness. And even though I feel kind of bad for Mr. Parrish, I'm also really glad that Athena's dad stood up for her like that.

Mr. Cronusson hears my giggle and looks over at me. "Ah. It is the Fanny child."

Sometimes he calls me "The Fanny Child." I really, really, hate it, but there's not much I can do about it. Once I asked him to just call me Fanny.

Once.

"Um. Hi, Mr. Cronusson."

"And where were you when my daughter was punishing miscreants?"

"I was... there."

"And yet you did nothing."

He looks at me with such a cold, mean stare that I want to shrivel up and die. Because he's right. I didn't do anything. If it wasn't for Athena, who knows if Gemma would ever have gotten her glasses back?

I'll never be as gutsy as her, and the knowledge of it fills me with shame.

"I... meant to."

Mr. Cronusson scoffs. "Naturally. All of you MEAN to do things, don't you?"

All of us? All of us who? All of us kids? Sometimes Athena's dad says really weird things.

Mrs. Caldwell steps into the hallway and sees Mr. Cronusson talking to me. She sees that I'm upset. She frowns.

"Mr. Cronusson, is there anything you need with Fanny? Because she has to get back in the classroom now."

Mr. Cronusson rolls his eyes. "Of course. Go." He flicks his wrist at me like a haughty aristocrat dismissing a servant. I bet that's how he thinks of me. A lowly servant who's not good enough to hang out with his daughter.

Down the hall, Athena comes out of the principal's office, smiling like it's her birthday and it's time to eat cake. She waves at me, and I wave back, weakly.

"Fanny? Get back to your desk," says Mrs. Caldwell, but her voice is kind.

I go back to my desk and sit down next to Gemma. Some of the other kids are looking at me with curiosity, but I don't say anything. I try not to make eye contact with anybody.

"What happened?" Gemma whispers. Her eyes are big and curious.

"I'll tell you later."

Athena enters the classroom, and as she does, everyone bursts into applause. Well... everyone except Daniel, but that's to be expected.

Athena grins and does a little bow and a curtsy. She sits on the other side of me. She flicks her dark hair back and looks super cool.

Gemma leans back and peers around me, looking at Athena.

"Athena? Thanks."

Athena nods. "Don't mention it." She smiles and looks super proud of herself, which she is, and should be.

CHAPTER FOUR

I'm at Athena's house for dinner. I was worried about coming over, after the talk I had with her dad at school, but Athena said that her dad wouldn't be there because he has a date tonight.

I hate to admit how glad that made me feel. I want to like Mr. Cronusson, but he makes it really hard, because he's so haughty all the time. It's one of the things that makes me glad I have the dad I do. All my friends like my dad, because he's nice to them. He would never treat my friends like irritating servants.

Even with Mr. Cronusson gone, dinner at Athena's house is weird. Instead of sitting at a table, like normal people, they lie on these long couches, and her housekeeper brings us trays of food, and we lounge around eating, even though I worry about making a mess.

And if I made a mess, it would be a Big Deal, because the room where they eat is basically an art museum, with all these

41

statues and paintings and gorgeous tables that probably cost more than my whole house. If I spilled soup on the carpet, or smeared sauce on the furniture, it would ruin some priceless artifact, and my family would become homeless and bankrupt trying to repay the Cronussons. So, no pressure or anything, just eat your dinner.

"Don't worry about it," says Athena, whenever I express my concerns. "We do this all the time. Just try not to be messy."

She says it like it's that simple, but have you ever tried to eat soup while lying down? It's not as easy as you'd think, and you probably don't think it's that easy. At least it's not tomato soup, or borscht. It's a clear broth that would only leave a faint stain if I spilled it, which, thank goodness, I don't.

Of course, Athena never spills a drop. She props herself up on her elbow and expertly sips from her dainty little spoon. I try to imitate her as best I can.

"So who's your dad taking on a date?"

I try to imagine the kind of woman Mr. Cronusson would like. I bet he only dates extremely attractive women in tight body-con dresses, who get their hair done at expensive salons and wear mean-looking stilettos. Women who giggle a lot at his jokes—if he makes any—and act impressed by everything he says and does.

Athena smiles and shrugs. "Don't know. Some woman."

"Have you met her?"

"No, and I don't want to."

"Really? I'd be curious if it was my dad. I'd want to meet her."

I can't imagine my dad going on a date though. He goes on date nights with Mom sometimes, but they're kind of boring. Like, they just go see a movie and eat dinner. It's more like a hangout than a date. I try to imagine my dad, nervously getting dressed in his nicest clothes, planning something romantic for a woman who isn't my mom. It's hard to picture, but what I can picture is kind of sad and depressing.

But Mr. Cronusson is another story. He's not like my dad at all. He's intimidating and rich. I imagine his dates are more like "woman hunting" than romantic events. These women must have nerves of steel, obviously.

Athena sets down her spoon. "Yeah. The thing is, with my dad... he goes on a lot of dates, with a lot of women. And sometimes it gets serious, but mostly it's..."

She trails off, and I try to understand what it must be like for her. My parents are still married, but if they weren't, and my dad dated a lot of women, I don't know how I'd react or how I'd feel. I don't think I'd feel great about it.

Athena continues. "It doesn't end well, when he gets involved with women."

I nod and try to seem like a sophisticated friend who understands all about men and their dating habits. The truth is, I've never had a boyfriend. Or a kiss. Or even held hands. So, I am not qualified to give advice on this subject. But I am curious.

"Would you like it if it did work out? I mean, would you like to have a mom?"

We never talk about it, but Athena doesn't have a mom. At first, I assumed that her parents were divorced, and her mom just lived somewhere far away, but when I asked her about it, she said that her dad had never been married, and that she had never met her mom.

I think her mom must have died in childbirth or something, like an old-fashioned prairie woman, but I know better than to pressure Athena to talk about it. I bet it's very painful for her.

"No, I don't want a mother. It would make things too complicated."

I think about that, and I decide she's right. A new mom would have lots of new rules, new preferences, new ideas about how things should be. Athena's whole life would change. And, despite her scary dad, her life is pretty awesome. I wouldn't want it to change either, if I were her. She's got it pretty good.

But then again, what if she wound up with a mom like mine? My mom isn't perfect, but she loves me and takes care of me. I think that kind of mom would be good for Athena. I bet a good mom would take the edge off her dad's scariness.

"So after dinner, I think we should practice for the pageant," says Athena, all no-nonsense and business-like.

"Ok."

I'm still surprised she wants to be in the pageant. It's just not her.

The housekeeper comes and takes away the soup bowls and brings in the next course, which is pasta with olives, feta, and tomatoes. It's delicious, and it's what I always request when I come for dinner.

I know it sounds bad that I keep calling her "the house-keeper" instead of her name, but the truth is, Athena's dad is always hiring and firing housekeepers, and it's difficult to keep track of them. I think this one has only been working here for a week or so. I wonder if she thinks it's weird to serve us on couches like this. I bet she does.

"But you know, we can do something else. I know the pageant isn't really your thing," I say.

"Don't be silly," she says. "I want to see what song you're gonna sing. I'll coach you. And you can help me pick out which paintings to show."

My heart constricts. Athena's paintings are perfect. Like, professionally perfect. She could sell them in an art gallery and become a famous artist and retire to the south of France. In fact, that's probably what she's going to do, when she grows up.

"Are you sure you want to show your paintings for talent?"

I blurted it before I could stop myself, and now I flinch.

Athena frowns at me. "Yes. Why wouldn't I?"

"I just mean, it's... you don't like pageants. Why would you, you know... exploit your art, or whatever?"

Her face softens. "Oh, I see what you mean. No, it's ok. In fact, I have an idea. Come with me."

I follow Athena up to her bedroom.

Side note: I love Athena's bedroom. It's all gleaming white with royal blue and gold accents. It is huge, bigger than half of my house, and it has its own bathroom, and its own gigantic flat-screen TV, and curtains around the bed, like a princess would have.

She opens up her closet and brings out a few paintings and sets them on her bed, so we can view them all together.

They're all paintings of women, some of whom I recognize, some I don't.

"Here we have Marie Curie, Ada Lovelace, Hypatia, Mary Shelley, and Lucille Ball."

"These are great!" I say, and I mean it.

"Thank you. But more importantly, they are all geniuses. Women who succeeded because of their intellect and skill. Not because of their beauty."

"I don't know," I say, looking at one of the paintings, "Lucille Ball was really pretty."

"Yes, but that wasn't the point of her," says Athena. She fingers the painting lovingly. "That's not why she was successful. She wasn't just an ornament." She looks at me and smiles. "If I'm going to be in a pageant, I want to infuse it with a little feminism. It's the least I can do. What do you think?"

I look at the paintings for a minute. Each woman looks straight out at me, like she's taking my measure and finding me wanting. I feel like each of them is judging me, telling me I'll never be smart enough to compete with them.

Or the girl who painted them.

"I think it's a great idea," I say softly.

Athena grins. "Awesome. I think so too." She gathers up

47

the paintings.

"Now. What song are you going to sing?"

Of course, I've thought about this a lot. The obvious choice would be "Life of Ice," but I think for the pageant I need something a little more flashy and upbeat. Something that shows what a fun, sassy girl I am. Something I can belt out with a smile.

"'I Hope She Will Try', by Natalie Dark," I say, proud of my choice.

Athena's eyes widen, and she looks skeptical. "Whoa. Really?"

A sudden flash of anger shoots through me, down to my fingertips.

"Yes, really. Why?"

"It's just... that's a really hard song to sing. I mean, Natalie Dark said in an interview that she only performs that song like, once a year, because it's so rough on her voice."

"So? I'm not gonna perform it every day, Athena. Just this once, for the pageant."

"Ok, ok," says Athena, holding up her hands in an "I surrender" pose. "It's a cool song."

"Yes, it is," I say, slightly mollified. I don't know why she's being so negative.

"So let's hear it," she says.

"Right now?"

"Yeah. We need to practice, right? So let's practice."

She's right, of course.

I sigh and move to the center of the room, as if I'm taking the stage. This room is big enough that it probably has great acoustics, but I can't be sure, since I've never sung in here before. I roll my shoulders back and breathe from my diaphragm. I open my mouth to sing.

And then I stop.

Athena is holding up her phone, recording me!

"Hey, what are you doing?"

She frowns.

"I'm recording you. This is how you get better. You watch yourself and listen to yourself, and then you know what to improve."

Just the sight of that camera pointed at me makes me feel dizzy. My face flushes hot and cold.

"You can't... you can't record me."

"Why not?"

"Because... because you just can't."

"Fanny, what's wrong?"

"It freaks me out, ok?"

Athena puts the phone down.

"You know I wouldn't show it to anyone, right? It's just for us to watch."

"I know that, it just... I don't know what's wrong with me. I need to get over this. Ok. You can record me. Just... let me turn around so I can't see you recording me."

I think that might work. Out of sight, out of mind.

But Athena sighs.

"Fanny, if you can't handle this, how are you going to handle the pageant?"

"I DON'T KNOW!"

Athena is shocked by my outburst, and I'm embarrassed.

"I'm sorry. I'm just... nervous."

Athena stands up and approaches me. She hugs me. And when she lets go... I don't know. I feel different.

I'm not nervous anymore. In fact, I kind of want her to record me. I want her to record me and send that video out to the world. I want it to be a viral YouTube sensation. I want Beyoncé to see it and call me and ask me to collaborate with her on this new song she's been working on, and then we become friends, and then I get a record deal, and then my life is perfect, forever.

"Feel better?" Athena asks.

"Actually, yeah. It's... weird."

"Sometimes you just need a hug," she says, briskly. Then she picks up her phone and hits record.

And just like that, I can sing.

CHAPTER FIVE

Last night was such a great success, I'm going to go to Athena's again tonight, to practice again. After I got rid of my nerves, it was like magic! I sang my heart out, and better yet, I didn't get uncomfortable watching the video of myself, like I thought I would. Instead, it was informative, and it really helped me to improve my routine. Even Athena was impressed.

It's after school now, and Athena, Gemma and I are headed toward Athena's house. It's a nice day, a perfect day for a walk. Breezy, not too humid. A delicate white butterfly floats near my head and settles on a rose bush. The roses are fragrant and warm in the sun. A little baby owl hoots at us from a tree, and it makes me smile.

Wait, an owl?

"Hey, guys, look in that tree. It's a baby owl."

I point at the owl.

Athena and Gemma look up. It's a little snowy white owl, all fluffy and big-eyed. I want to snatch it out of the tree and snuggle it, but of course, I won't. You're not supposed to cuddle wildlife.

"Oh hey, it is. Cool," says Gemma.

"I mean, isn't it kind of weird though? Aren't owls usually only awake at night?" I ask.

"I don't think so," says Athena—and the way she says it makes me pause. She says it quickly, like she's nervous or something.

"Yeees. That's where they got the expression 'night owl,'" I say, unsure why I have to explain this.

"I think that's only some owls," says Athena, nodding curtly.

"Let's google it," says Gemma, taking out her phone.

"No!"

Gemma and I look at Athena, puzzled.

"Why not?" Gemma asks.

"Because... because it's gone. It probably wasn't even an owl. It was some other kind of bird."

I look up into the tree, and sure enough, the owl is gone. It just disappeared.

"I'm sure it was an owl," I say.

"RETARD!"

All three of us spin around, trying to find who shouted

that. Across the street, a window slams shut quickly, and the blinds sway. It came from the blue house, the one with old, battered looking steps.

"Was that..." I ask.

Athena's eyes narrow.

"I think it was."

"Coward," I mutter.

Gemma looks really upset. I lean over and pat her on the shoulder.

"Just ignore him. He's a total douche nozzle."

Athena shakes her head.

"We can't ignore it. Bullies like him, they only get worse unless someone teaches them some manners. I've seen it before. It's always the same."

I want to ask her what she means by that, but she's already striding across the street, banging on Daniel's door. The door is white, with lots of chips in the paint, and flakes float off of it when Athena bangs on it.

Of course, the coward doesn't answer.

"What if his parents answer the door?" I worry, thinking how awkward that would be.

"So?" Gemma crosses her arms over her chest. "Then we

can tell them what a jerk their son is."

I guess Gemma doesn't care if it's awkward or not, which I guess is fair, since she's the one who is being called the R word.

"IF YOU DON'T OPEN UP, I'M COMING IN!" Athena yells. Her voice is loud and authoritative. She sounds like a general, commanding her soldiers to go do battle in some very bloody war.

Athena is banging and shouting, and I know she's serious. She will break down that door.

Apparently, Daniel understands this about her, because he opens the door... holding a baseball bat. He's wearing his usual sweatpants and badly fitting t-shirt, but that baseball bat makes me take him a lot more seriously.

"Athena, back away!" I shout.

I know Athena is brave, and is capable of handling herself. But I also know that Daniel has a freaking baseball bat. I once watched a TV show where a man beat another man to death with a baseball bat covered in barbed wire. It was super messed-up, and I don't want to see anything remotely like that ever again, as long as I live.

"Oh, so you're a big tough man with a baseball bat, huh?" Athena taunts.

"Get off my property!" he shouts. He holds the bat like he's about to hit a pitch and steps toward her.

Athena doesn't flinch.

"You spoke disrespectfully to my friend," she says.

"So?"

"So, you need to apologize."

"I'm not apologizing for anything."

"Yes, you are, or you'll be sorry."

Athena points at Gemma.

"That girl is one of the most intelligent, awesome, adorable people on the planet, and when you call her that terrible word, it makes us all sick to our stomachs. So you apologize to her, to Fanny, and to me."

"I SAID GET OFF MY LAWN!"

Daniel lunges at Athena with his baseball bat, and I run forward. I have to help, I have to save her. I'm not sure what my plan is, but I know that I can NOT let her get hit by that bat.

But then, Daniel is gone. His bat clatters to the concrete steps, loud and unnerving. The clothes he was wearing lie in a pile on the ground, a disturbing puddle of gray and blue.

"Oh no!" Athena wails. She pulls at her pretty hair. She looks around, frantic.

"Um, where's Daniel?" I ask. I rush closer to see what's going on.

From behind me, Gemma shouts, "UM, WHAT JUST HAPPENED?"

Athena is pacing, looking at the ground. "Oh no, oh no, oh no. Ok,. I can fix this."

I'm standing next to Athena now, and I see what she's seeing. It's a cockroach. A large, brown, ugly cockroach. But it's different than other cockroaches. This one has brown hair on its head. Brown hair that looks just like Daniel's.

"Um... Athena?" I point at the roach.

"Hey, guys?" Gemma asks.

"Gemma, come look at this!" I shout.

"No! Stay back, Gemma! I have to concentrate."

Her face is panicked, and her eyes are twitching. I think it's gonna be hard for her to concentrate on anything at all, until she calms down.

"Concentrate on what?" I ask.

"I have to turn him back."

"But... Athena... what are you saying? Is this... is that... is that Daniel?"

Athena turns to me and takes my shoulders. "I'm so sorry

Fanny. You were never supposed to see anything like this. I can't believe I was so careless, that I made such a stupid mistake."

I look at the cockroach, which appears to be in great distress. It is spinning in circles, waving its little antennae like it's begging for help. It's really sad. I kind of want to help it, but I'm not sure how, or if it's a good idea to touch it.

"So... how did you do that? Are you a witch or something?"

Gemma has crossed the street now and is looking at the cockroach too.

"Whoa! Cool! It has hair!"

Athena and I look at her like she's lost her mind.

She shrugs. "What? It's cool."

The cockroach is flicking his wings, furiously. He is clearly agitated.

"Alright, never mind," says Athena. "I'm gonna turn him back, and once that's done, we'll all go to my house, and I'll explain everything. I just need you both to stay calm until then, ok?"

"Ok," we both agree. And somehow, I manage to actually stay calm. Or, at least, I don't run away, or pass out, or scream, even though I kind of feel like doing all of those things.

The cockroach lifts off the ground and flies away.

"Wait, no! Come back! Daniel, I can fix this! COME BACK!"

Athena's shouts do not bring Daniel back, though. He is gone.

Athena sits down and hyperventilates. I sit down next to her and try to get her to breathe. I tell her to put her head between her knees.

"Deep breaths. That's right. Deep breaths," I say, using my most soothing voice.

Eventually she can breathe well enough to talk again, but then she starts crying.

"I can't believe I did that. And now he's gone. Who knows where he went? I'll never find him now. This is not good. This is so not good."

"It's Ok, Athena. We'll find him, and... and everything will be alright. Can you use your... magic to find him?"

"No, I don't have that kind of power," she sniffs.

"Well maybe it's for the best," says Gemma.

I glare at her. She is not helping.

"Well, maybe it is," Gemma insists, seeing my look. "He was a jerk, and probably a psychopath. He would have probably grown up to, like, kidnap little kids and sew quilts out of their hair or something."

"Gemma, stop it!" I command.

"What? I'm saying that we're all better off now. It's called being comforting!"

I'm ready to tell Gemma off, but Athena lifts her head and stands up. She takes a deep breath. She looks at us, all nervous. It's weird. I never see her nervous. It's like seeing an octopus with a flamethrower, all wrong and out of place.

"Alright. My secret's out, I guess. So, let's go to my house. I'll explain everything, and once I've explained, we can make a plan to fix this."

"Sounds good," I agree, even though it doesn't sound good, it sounds hard and confusing, and not like something I want to do, at all. But I'm confused, and scared, and I know we need to have a talk about this, so I agree.

"Sure," says Gemma. I can tell from her face that she feels the same as me. I give her a look of sympathy, and she nods back at me.

Then, together, we set off for Athena's house. At least it's a nice day for a walk.

CHAPTER SIX

We can't go into Athena's bedroom, because there is no elevator or ramp, and we can't carry Gemma up the stairs. So we have to sit in the living room, which is cold, and spotless, and intimidating. I wonder if Athena could use her magic to lift Gemma upstairs, but now is not the time to ask. I'm still really confused about what just happened, and I need information.

Also, I JUST FOUND OUT THAT MY FRIEND CAN DO MAGIC.

I don't know about Gemma, but I'm on edge. I mean, we just saw a kid get turned into a cockroach. By our friend. It shouldn't be possible, but somehow it is. Are we hallucinating? Am I hallucinating? Have I gone crazy? Am I in a mental hospital, right now, mumbling about cockroaches and staring at the ceiling?

"First of all, you're not crazy," says Athena, reading my mind. "I did turn that boy into a cockroach. And I'm sorry about that."

"But how? How did you do it?" My voice is high-pitched and a little hysterical. I take a deep breath. I need to get it together.

Athena sighs and stands up. She paces back and forth, like a tiger in a cage. "This is really hard. Ok. First of all, my name is Athena."

I look at Gemma. She is furrowing her brows, and I can feel myself doing the same thing.

Athena giggles, nervous.

"Yeah, I know, you know that. Ok. My dad's name... is Zeus."

That name rings a bell.

"Like the Greek god?" I ask.

Athena is overjoyed. "Yes! Yes, exactly! So you see?"

She holds out her hands to us, pleading for us to understand. But I don't, not really.

"Ok..."

"Zeus, son of Cronus," Athena continues. "And we live in Athens. Not the real Athens, but still, Athens. My dad thought that was pretty funny, when we... moved here."

"Why is that funny?" Gemma asks, and I'm wondering the same thing.

"You know, because... this is harder than I thought it would be. Alright, I'm just gonna come out with it. I'm a goddess."

I roll my eyes. "No need for false modesty," I say.

"No, I mean, an actual goddess. I'm the goddess, Athena."

I look at Gemma, who is gaping at Athena with wide eyes.

"That makes so much sense!" Gemma says. "The magic, and how good you are at everything, and how smart you are. It makes so much sense!"

"Wait, you believe this?" I ask.

Gemma looks at me like I'm insane. "Don't you?"

I throw my hands up in the air.

"I don't know! I don't know what I think."

Athena sits down on the floor and looks up at us. Her eyes are hopeful, and watery, like she's ready to cry, which makes me feel bad.

"I know this is hard to believe, but it's true. You saw the cockroach with your own eyes. And there are other things."

"Like what?" I ask.

"Well... the owls. You saw that one today, right?"

I nod.

"That's not the only one. Owls follow me around everywhere. They're kind of... kind of a spirit animal, I guess you'd call it? I don't know the right term. Haven't you noticed them?"

"You said that wasn't an owl," I say, flatly. I'm kind of annoyed. Was she trying to make me think I was crazy? Was she gaslighting me, like an abusive boyfriend? Not cool.

"I know, and I'm sorry. I just didn't want you to... I don't know. I'm not supposed to tell anyone about my... goddess-ness. I didn't want you to get suspicious."

"I wouldn't have assumed you're a goddess, just because I saw an owl. I'm not a crazy person," I grumble.

Athena chuckles. "I guess not, but I'm supposed to be careful. Which is why this cockroach thing is not good, not at all. My dad is gonna kill me. I mean, he might literally kill me."

That's a little dramatic. I mean, sure, Zeus is scary, but he wouldn't murder his child!

But then again, she's not a child, is she? She's not even human. And neither is he. They probably don't have a typical father–daughter relationship.

This is all so weird.

"So wait," Gemma pipes up. "If you're a goddess, you must be really old, right? Why are you eleven? I mean, why are you living as a kid? Shouldn't you be on Mount Olympus or whatever?"

Athena nods solemnly. "Yes, that is where I should be. But thousands of years ago, we were thrown out."

Gemma is aghast. "What? Why? How is that possible?"

Athena runs a hand through her glossy hair. "It's a long story. But basically, in order for a god or goddess to have power, we need people to believe that we have power. It's like... if you were the President of the United States. You're only the President because people believe you're the President and allow you to hold that job. If I said I was the President, that wouldn't make me the President, because no one believes that I am. Does that make sense?"

"Kind of," I say. "So... if nobody believes that you're a goddess, then you don't get to be a goddess?"

Athena shakes her head, frustrated. "I'm not explaining this very well. The way the pantheon worked, in Ancient Greece, we had these temples. A temple for each god or goddess. As long as we had worshippers, we could live in those temples. People would bring us food and wine, and gifts. We had parties. It was really nice."

Athena's eyes are focused far away, like she's no longer in the room with us. "But people stopped coming. Or rather, they stopped believing. And when that happened, we lost our temples... and our immortal bodies."

"So, you're mortal now," says Gemma. "Like, you can die and rot in the ground, just like everybody else."

"Yes, but there's a catch," says Athena. "Every time we die, we get reborn, into new bodies."

"Whoa," says Gemma. "So you're reincarnated. That's so cool!"

Athena smiles wryly. "Kind of. Except we aren't born into baby bodies, like other kinds of reincarnation. We sort of... take over the bodies of whatever people have recently vacated theirs."

"I'm sorry... what?" I can't believe this. Just a minute ago, I found out that my best friend is a goddess. Now she's telling me that she's a body snatcher, too? What else is she? A fairy? Santa Claus?

"I know, I know how it sounds. But, you know, people die all the time. And when a person dies, we just sort of... help ourselves to their physical bodies. That way we can continue to live."

I can't take this sitting down anymore. I need to move around. I'm too amped up from all this. I stand and walk around the giant living room, not even worried about smashing a vase or a statue, like I normally do.

"Well, what if you don't die together?" Gemma asks. "Do you get separated?"

Athena nods. "Yes. When our mortal bodies die, we go to The Isles of the Blessed. If there's another god or goddess there, we can try to find bodies that died together, so we can live together on earth. It's easier. The last time I died, my dad happened to be there at the same time, so we found a father and daughter who died together and we took their bodies."

"Isles of the Blessed?" Gemma asks. "What's that?"

"It's nice. It's a place where we can stay and recharge before being reborn. Sort of like a resort for the dead."

My head is spinning.

"Wow. So this body you have, this is some girl who died? And same with your dad? That is so freaking cool," says Gemma.

Athena shrugs and smiles, but she looks kind of uncomfortable about getting praised for body snatching.

"So is that how you got this house? And all this stuff? You stole the bodies of some rich people? Oh my god! You're like black widows!" Gemma's eyes are flashing and eager.

Sometimes Gemma gives me the creeps.

"Well, no," says Athena. "These bodies died somewhere else. Juneau, Alaska, I think? Whenever we get reborn, another god or goddess helps us out with money, until we can manage on our own. This time my uncle gave us a bunch of treasure and set us up in this house. He's a deep-sea treasure hunter."

"Oh my god, this just gets cooler and cooler," says Gemma. "Where does he live? Can we meet him? Can we go treasure

69

hunting with him?"

Gemma might be impressed, but I'm freaked out. I don't know how to process all this, or what to think.

"So, let me get this straight," I say. Gemma and Athena are watching me, like I'm a rabid raccoon approaching their food stash. "You, Athena, are actually the goddess Athena. Your dad is the god, Zeus. You are no longer allowed on Mount Olympus, or at your Greek temple, because people stopped believing in you, so now you have to live in human bodies. Which is why you live in Athens, Georgia, in the body of an eleven-year-old girl."

Athena takes a deep breath.

"Yes."

"Yes?"

"Yes. That's it."

"But that doesn't make sense," I say.

"What doesn't make sense?"

"If you're not a goddess anymore, how come you have powers? Shouldn't you be just, like... ordinary?"

She shrugs and smiles. "I don't know. I guess we still get to retain some of the perks of our former lives. Like, have you heard of Dionysus?"

I shake my head, frustrated. I look at Gemma, who

shrugs. She doesn't know either. I hate not knowing things.

"Well, he was the god of wine and partying. Now, he's the owner of Shooting Star Vineyards. He's actually my brother, technically."

I stare at her blankly.

"You know, Shooting Star Vineyards? The largest producer of red wines in the United States? He uses his powers to do what he was made to do. Lots of the old gods are doing the same thing."

"And you? What do you do?"

"What do you mean?"

"I mean, what do you do? What are you the goddess of?"

She straightens up. "Wisdom, courage, inspiration, civilization, law, justice, strategic warfare, mathematics, strength, arts and crafts, and general skill."

"Oh, is that all?" Gemma asks dryly, waving a dismissive hand.

And that sets me off. I start laughing. And so does Gemma. And finally, so does Athena, and we're all laughing at the absurdity of all this.

When we finish laughing, Athena brings things back to order.

"Look, I'm really happy you guys know about this. It's been hard to keep this secret for so long, from so many people."

"Are we the only ones who know?"

Athena nods.

I feel a warm glow, knowing that we're special, privy to secret knowledge. It's kind of like being in a secret society, or an exclusive club.

"But the thing is, we still have a problem."

I nod. "The cockroach," I say.

"Yes. We really need to find him so we can turn him back into Daniel. Even if cockroach IS an improvement over his original personality."

"So, how do we find him?" Gemma asks.

"I don't know," says Athena. "I was hoping you two might have some ideas."

"Us?" I blurt. "You're a freaking goddess! Can't you use your goddess powers to locate him? Like some kind of magic GPS tracking?"

She shakes her head.

"It doesn't work like that. I'm not omniscient. I can't see everything, and I don't know everything, and I can't find things that are lost any better than you can."

"Well. That's not good," I say.

"No. No, it is not," Athena agrees.

Gemma tilts her head, thinking.

"Well, maybe it's not as hard as we're making it. I mean, where do cockroaches like to go? We just have to hunt for cockroach nests, and see if we can find him. Plus, he has hair, so he'll stand out from the other cockroaches."

"You make it sound like this is an easy thing to do," I point out, "but there are like, millions of cockroaches in the world, and they hide in buildings and cupboards and stuff. It's not gonna be easy to find him."

"Do you have a better idea?" Gemma asks.

"Well... no."

Athena stands up and claps her hands together.

"Well, alright then. I guess Operation Cockroach Hunt is a go. So, I'm gonna need you two to do some research. Let's find a list of restaurants that have health code violations. That's as good a place to start as any."

"And make lists of dirty houses and apartment buildings in our neighborhoods," I suggest.

"Yeah. And let's search places that are near Daniel's house first. I mean, he probably didn't go far, right?" Gemma asks.

"Good thinking," says Athena.

Gemma is already headed for the door, ready to get started on her research, but I don't get up just yet. There's one more question I have for Athena.

"Athena?" I begin, softly, so Gemma can't hear. "You're my best friend. Why didn't you tell me?"

Athena presses her lips together, like she's in pain.

"I couldn't."

I nod and move toward the door, ready to leave. But then I turn around. I have one more thing to say.

"You could have trusted me," I say.

Athena spreads her hands out hopelessly.

I nod and turn away.

CHAPTER SEVEN

By the time I get home, everyone in town knows about Daniel's disappearance, including my mom, which explains why she grabs me as soon as I walk in the door, like I've just returned from war or something. She hugs me so tightly I'm pretty sure it damages my intestines. "Honey, I'm so glad you're home. Where were you?"

"Athena's. Remember? I told you where I was gonna be."

"A boy's gone missing! I had no idea where you were! I was terrified."

This is what happens when a kid goes missing. Your mom completely forgets about any conversations you had earlier in the day, because all she can think about is the fact that a kid is missing, and it scrambles her brains.

"I'm sorry you were worried, Mom. But... um... a boy's gone missing, you say?"

I'm such a bad actress.

"Yes! It's all over the news. I got an Amber alert just a few minutes ago. His name was Daniel Doyle. I think they said he went to your school. Do you know this boy?"

I panic inside. What am I supposed to say? "Yeah, I know him, and he's a total douche nozzle, and Athena turned him into a cockroach, but it's ok. We're working on it."

No. I cannot say that to my mom. Instead, I will deny everything.

"No."

"Really?"

I can tell that my mom doesn't believe me. She has that skeptical look on her face that she gets when I lie. Probably because I'm a terrible liar. I can't look her in the eyes, and my face turns bright red. It's the worst.

"I mean yes. He goes to my school, but we're not friends. I don't know him very WELL."

That's the truth, anyway.

Mom exhales, but she still looks worried. Her forehead is extra wrinkly. It reminds me of the time when our dog Millie got really sick, and we had to take her to the veterinarian over and over, and the doctor said there was a surgery we could do, but it would cost like three thousand dollars, and Mom was so stressed out, because she didn't know what to do. She has that same look on her face right now.

"His mother says she knows that he came home from school. He'd eaten a snack and left his dishes on the coffee table. But then he just... disappeared. They're saying it's a possible kidnapping."

I swallow hard. I haven't thought about Daniel's mother until just now. She must be so scared, so upset. Even though Daniel is the worst, his mom probably loves him. She probably loves him a lot, just like my mom loves me.

Mom sees I'm upset and throws her arms around me in another boa constrictor hug.

"Oh honey, don't worry. Nobody's going to kidnap you, I promise. You're safe at home now."

I let her hug me, accepting the comfort, even though she has no idea why I'm really upset. I get a sudden urge to tell her everything, to tell her the whole story about Athena and her dad and the cockroach. It would feel so good to get everything off my chest.

But of course, I don't tell her. She would never believe me, and even if she did, she wouldn't be able to help. Best case scenario, I'd be in the same position I'm in now.

Worst case scenario, I get sent to a special hospital where

they attach electrodes to my brain and fry it. Or they stick an ice pick in my nose and scramble my head up, until I can't talk about cockroaches anymore, and can't even remember my name.

Ok, that probably wouldn't happen. But still.

"I'm gonna go up to my room now. I've got some research to do."

It's a relief to say something to my mom that isn't a lie.

———————

Athena calls the Mathmagicians meeting to order, her face tight and tired, wearing her comfy track suit, which she never wears in public except when she's exercising, because she says a lady doesn't wear athleisure unless engaged in athletics. She looks like she didn't get much sleep last night, which she probably didn't. Neither did I.

We haven't had an opportunity to talk all day, which is difficult, because it's very hard to plan a search and rescue operation when nobody will let you communicate. First, it was standardized test day, so everyone had to be silent all day, or risk being accused of cheating. Then, I had to leave at lunch for a dentist's appointment, so we couldn't talk then, either. I sat in the dentist's chair, clenching my fists, trying hard to be still, but it was really hard, because my brain was racing around, and I had no way to make it slow down. It felt like I was in that chair FOREVER.

Now, finally, we are at the math club meeting, and still we can't talk, because there are people all around! Math club has twelve members right now, and that's way too many people. We are all seated at the same long table, so it's easy to hear other people talking. Usually, I like the long table, because it feels like we're all hanging out together at a pizza place or something, but today I hate this long table.

But, of course, Athena has a solution.

"I was thinking that today we could partner up and do some fractals. Just for fun."

Murmurs of approval go up all around. Everybody loves fractals.

Athena grabs my hand and leads me to a small table in the corner, while the other students start their projects. She grabs a big thick book about fractals, opens it, and sits down in front of it, pretending to study. I sit down next to her. We speak in whispers, so nobody can hear us.

"Have you been able to talk to Gemma?" I ask.

Gemma is not in the Mathmagicians. She says it's "totally geeky" and "not fun," but I think she's just bad at math and too embarrassed to admit it. Which is silly. Athena and I would never make fun of her; in fact, we would help her until she was just as good as us, and then we could all do math club together, and go on a trip to Hawaii, and someday form a globetrotting society for genius mathematicians. And maybe solve crimes.

Anyway.

"No, I haven't had a chance," says Athena. "But I do have a plan."

I sigh with relief. I'm glad one of us does, because my research was not very productive. As it turns out, the internet isn't a great source of information on how to find a cockroach-boy and transform him into a human boy, or how to reverse spells cast by Greek goddesses.

She pulls a hand-drawn map out of her backpack and lays it on the table. She's drawn a picture of Daniel's house, and the surrounding houses and streets and businesses. It's really impressive, of course. There's a little scale drawn in the bottom corner, and a key, and even a beautifully sketched compass star. Seriously, you could hang this map up on the wall, like art. She must have used India ink or something fancy.

She also has some printed pages on cockroaches, and their flight speed, mating habits, eating preferences, etc. The pages are organized into a binder, with labels. I flip through the pages, and see that she's scrawled notes in the margins, things like "temperature on Saturday?" And "take wingspan into account when calculating flight speeds."

Athena talks while I look through the binder.

"So, according to Professor Google, cockroaches can't actually fly very well, or for very long distances. So if Daniel only flew, he wouldn't be too far from his home."

"That's great!"

"Yeah, except it's unlikely that he didn't at least try to run. Cockroaches can run really, really fast. Like three miles per hour!"

"That's not that fast," I protest. Sometimes I use my mom's treadmill, and three miles per hour is just, like, a fast walk. It doesn't even make me tired unless I set it at a really high incline, like I'm walking up a really steep hill.

"It is if you're only an inch or two long."

"Oh. Right."

"It's been twenty-five hours since he got transformed, so I figure he probably couldn't have got more than seventy-five miles away from his house."

"Seventy-five miles! We can't search that much area!"

I imagine us trying to cover that much area on foot, after school. I'm pretty sure my feet would fall off. And it's not like we could ask our parents to drive us. I try to imagine what my parents would say if I asked them to drive me seventy-five miles while I look for a hairy cockroach. I'm guessing they would say no.

"Well, I don't think we'll have to. It seems unlikely that he would just run for twenty-five hours without stopping. In fact, I have a feeling he would stay close to home."

I remember how fast he ran away, and I feel my heart sink.

"I don't know, he seemed pretty scared, like he wanted to get as far away as possible."

"He wanted to get away from ME," Athena protests, "not his house. I'm guessing as soon as we left, he went back home. I mean, that's what I'd do, in his position."

I frown, thinking about this. It makes a lot of sense. If I got turned into a bug, or anything else really, I'd want to stay someplace familiar, someplace where I felt safe.

"So, you think he's still himself? Like, inside? Or is he just a full-on cockroach now?"

It's actually a weird thought. If his brain is a cockroach brain, can he have human thoughts? What are cockroach thoughts like? I bet they don't think about much other than food and which predators to avoid. But a boy-turned-cockroach might be able to think about more complex things.

She shrugs. "When I transform, I still keep my same

brain and personality."

"YOU CAN TRANSFORM?"

I forgot to whisper, and I look around, ashamed of my outburst.

"Shhh! Keep it down."

"I know. I'm sorry."

"And yes, I can transform."

"Into a cockroach?"

I hope she can turn into a cockroach. That will make finding Daniel much easier, I imagine.

"No. An owl."

"An owl? What is with you and the owls?"

"I don't know," she whisper-snaps. "It's just one of those things."

"So you can turn other people into cockroaches, or whatever you want, but you can only turn yourself into an owl."

"Yes."

"This is so weird."

"I know. I'm sorry about all this. Really."

I pat her hand. "It's ok. It's not your fault."

She smiles at me. "So, I'm thinking we'll have a sleepover at your house, and we'll sneak out tonight and go find him."

"You think we should wait until tonight?"

That seems like a bad idea to me. The sooner we find him, the better. We don't want to wait until he gets eaten by a cat or something.

Athena nods.

"Yes. If we go to Daniel's house during the daytime, people will see us, and wonder why we're snooping around. Also, cockroaches are active at night. That's when they come out of hiding. They hide from daylight."

I actually kind of like the idea of sneaking out at night. It makes me feel dangerous. "We'll be sneaky, like burglars!"

Maybe we'll get really good at night-time sneakiness. Maybe we'll form a posse and do jewel heists. Maybe we'll steal back art that was stolen by the Nazis and return it to its rightful owners. We'll be burglar-vigilantes. We'll be super cool, and pretty, and really smart and intimidating.

Athena laughs. "Sounds perfect."

CHAPTER EIGHT

But first, we have to go to the Junior Miss Super Pretty Pageant orientation meeting.

That's where we are now. We're at the Mammoth Concert Hall, which is our community theater. They do classic plays like "The Odd Couple" and "Godspell." They also host the Junior Miss Super Pretty Pageant every year.

The building is old and musty, and smells like it's about two-hundred-years old, which I think it actually is. The seats are uncomfortable and stained. But the stage is beautiful, with a thick velvet purple curtain, and I long to get up on it and sing my heart out.

You know, after everyone has gone home.

It seems wrong to sit here talking about dresses and smiles and music when Daniel is a terrified cockroach, and everyone is worried about him. But what can I do? Athena is right. We have to wait.

Mrs. Harris is standing on the stage, smiling and welcoming us to the pageant. She assures us that this will be one of the most special and memorable experiences of our lives.

Two other adults are here, Mr. Garrison and Mr. Pacheco. They are going to be judges, and they watch us with appraising eyes. They are both old, like grandpa age. I wonder if they're always the judges, or if they choose new judges every year. I wonder how you qualify to be a beauty pageant judge. Do you have to take a test or something? Or is it just whoever volunteers? I wonder why these men volunteered.

Athena sits next to me, and she is tense. I know she doesn't like this, and I wonder again why she's insisting on doing it. I know she says it's because we're friends and she wants to be supportive, but she could be supportive from the audience. I wonder if there's something she's not telling me.

Mrs. Harris is talking, wearing yet another suit. I think that's just how she likes to dress, which is weird.

"Now, girls, if you'll all turn to page seven in your packets, we can start talking about the pageant itself."

I flip through my packet, which is just a bunch of rules and explanations. Page seven is titled "The Night of the Pageant" and it has little stars and hearts decorating it. There is a picture of a bunch of girls, all dressed in tulle skirts, dancing in a line, with big smiles on their faces.

"As you can see, the program begins at 7pm. We will start with our opening number, which will be a choreographed dance to 'Holding out for a Hero.'"

Athena snorts next to me, and I nudge her to be quiet. She gives me an innocent look, as if to say "what?" but I know she thinks the song is silly.

I actually kind of like that song.

"After the opening number, we will progress to the interview section of the evening. Each girl will come out onstage, and we will ask her a question, most likely about something that affects our community, our environment, or our world."

Mrs. Harris grins at us and wags a finger.

"But don't you worry too much about that. No one is expecting you to solve all the world's problems in this itty-bitty pageant. You just do your best, and remember, there are no wrong answers if you speak from your heart."

She thumps her chest with her hand, I guess to show what she means by "heart."

"Next, we'll move on to the talent portion, where each

of you can display your talents for the judges and your families to admire. Of course, we will need to approve your talent beforehand, to make sure it's in keeping with the high standards of this pageant, and to make sure we don't have any unpleasant incidents... like last year."

Athena and I look at each other. What happened last year? Did someone set their eyebrows on fire? Did someone have a seriously weird talent, like vomiting on command, or like, dog fighting?

I have to stifle a giggle, thinking about it.

Mrs. Harris continues.

"And then of course, we have the swimsuit round, where you all can put on your cutest swimsuits and show us all what a fun day at the beach is like for you!"

Athena raises her hand.

Oh no.

Mrs. Harris sees Athena, recognizes her, and frowns.

"Can we please hold all questions until the end of my presentation? Thank you."

Athena is not having that.

"No, Mrs. Harris, because what I have to say is important."

My heart wrenches in my chest. I've never heard a kid say that, to an adult. Just out loud, and confident. "What I have to say is important." God, I wish I could be like Athena. She makes it seem so easy.

Of course, she's a goddess. And she's had like a million years to practice. But still.

The other girls are whispering and looking at each other, more shocked than I am. Athena doesn't pay them any attention though. She's focused on what she wants to say.

"I refuse to participate in the swimsuit competition."

Mrs. Harris smiles tightly and says, "Well then, honey, you'll be disqualified from the pageant. All contestants must take part in all rounds in order to participate." She holds up her rule book. "It says so right here, on page two."

"Yes," says Athena, slowly, "but what if nobody participates in the swimsuit portion? Then what would happen? Would you cancel the pageant?"

"Young lady, if you have a problem with this pageant, I'm afraid I don't understand why you're here. Perhaps it would be better for you to find some other way to spend your time. Maybe soccer."

She tilts her head with a sickly sweet smile. It infuriates me, and it's not even aimed at me. I can't imagine how angry it must be making Athena.

But I don't have to imagine, because she shows us, right away.

Before I know what's happening, Athena is out of her seat, and ascending the stage. She snatches the microphone from Mrs. Harris, who gapes and clutches her pearls. I don't mean that as an expression, either. She literally clutches a string of pearls that she is wearing around her neck.

Athena pays her no attention, because she is Athena, and she is on a roll. She somehow looks taller than Mrs. Harris, though she must be a good foot shorter. Her gray eyes are narrowed and whip-smart. She is in her element.

"Girls," begins Athena, looking out at us, "you want to be in a beauty pageant. Great. There's nothing wrong with that. There's nothing wrong with wanting to sing and dance and be pretty. But the swimsuit portion of this contest IS wrong."

She turns and looks at the old man judges. Then she looks back at us.

"Your body is not an ornament. It's a tool. A tool for helping you live the life you want. And for these old men to make you take your clothes off, so they can judge whether or not they find your bodies attractive... well... it's gross."

There are murmurs as the girls next to me react to this speech.

Mrs. Harris takes the microphone away and glares at Athena. But Athena is not done talking. She just shouts louder.

"Girls! Join me in refusing to take part in the swimsuit portion of this pageant. Heck, even Miss America doesn't do swimsuit competitions anymore! It's an outdated, sexist and creepy tradition, and it needs to die!"

She looks at me straight in the eyes before she shouts—

"NO SWIMSUIT ROUND! NO SWIMSUIT ROUND! NO SWIMSUIT ROUND!"

Understanding my role, and what she wants me to do, I stand up and join her. Not only do I stand up, but I stand on the seat, even though it's one of those fold-up ones, and standing on it is totally not a safe thing to do.

"NO SWIMSUIT ROUND! NO SWIMSUIT ROUND! NO SWIMSUIT ROUND!"

I shake my fist in the air, to show I mean it, because I do. The idea of parading around in a swimsuit while judges discuss my body makes me feel sick and sweaty. There's no way I'm doing that if I don't have to.

Also, standing and shouting is actually pretty fun. It's not something I get to do very often.

And, like magic, all the girls around me start standing up

in their seats, too, chanting along with us.

The whole theater is alive with the sounds of fifth- and sixth- and seventh-grade girls shouting that they don't want to do a swimsuit round. And it's not just for the fun of shouting, either. I can tell that most of them really mean it. Athena has convinced them. She's convinced us all.

And just like that, the swimsuit competition is removed from the Junior Miss Super Pretty Pageant.

———————

After the pageant orientation, Athena and I walk toward my house. The weather is still great. It's fall, but summer is refusing to leave us. If it wasn't for the Halloween decorations, I'd never know it was October.

"That worked out well," says Athena.

I know she's talking about the swimsuit riot, and I nod in agreement.

"I'm pretty sure I'm not gonna win now though," she chuckles. "I don't think I made a great impression on the judges."

"Oh please," I snap. It comes out harsher than I meant it to.

Athena stops walking.

"Is something wrong?"

I sigh. "I just mean... you know you're gonna win. Obviously, you're gonna win."

"Why is that obvious?"

"Because you're a goddess! What the heck, Athena?"

"Oh, that." She waves her hand dismissively, like I said something silly. "That doesn't mean anything."

And that makes me angry, because it does mean something. And I want her to acknowledge that it does.

"Athena... you are a literal goddess, entering a beauty pageant with a bunch of ordinary kids. Don't you see how that's... I don't know. An unfair advantage?"

She looks hurt, and I backpedal. I don't want to hurt her feelings, but I need to make her understand somehow.

"I know you aren't going to like, cheat, or fix the competition or anything. I don't mean that kind of unfair. I just mean... I don't know what I mean."

She bites her lip and looks at me for a moment, in silence. Then, quietly, she says, "Did you ever think there might be a good reason for me to enter this pageant?"

"What do you mean? You said you didn't want me to do it alone. Is that not the reason?"

"Well, yes, that is the reason, kind of. But it's not..."

"What is it, Athena? What are you trying to tell me?"

She presses her lips together, like she's not sure if she

should say anything.

"Nothing. Forget it. Look, we need to get back to your house and get ready for tonight. We've got a bug to catch."

Before I can say anything else, she starts walking, and I know I won't get any more information out of her. At least, not right now.

CHAPTER NINE

Athena sleeps over at my house a lot. She has her own drawer with clothes in it, and her own toothbrush in our bathroom. My house is basically her second home, which makes no sense to me, because my room is waaaay less cool than hers. Why would she want to hang out here?

But tonight I'm glad, because it makes our mission a lot easier. First of all, I live closer to Daniel. Second, my parents are out for a date night, which means we can leave without anyone noticing.

But there's just one problem.

"How do you not have any black ski masks or leotards?" Athena demands, rifling through my closet.

"I don't know! I don't like to wear black."

I wonder if she's judging how common my clothes are. My mom always says it doesn't make sense to spend lots of money on clothes for a growing girl, since they'll all be too small for me before I get much wear out of them. So she buys all my clothes at cheap places, or secondhand stores. Athena's clothes are all designer labels, or specially tailored clothes that are made by her DAD'S PERSONAL TAILOR. Who has a personal tailor? Athena does. That's who.

But if Athena is grossed out by my wardrobe, she doesn't say anything about it. She's too focused on my distressing lack of burglar clothes.

"What do you mean you don't like to wear black? It's a classic color. It goes with everything."

"It doesn't go with my personality. Anyway, it's not like I knew this was gonna happen the last time I went shopping."

"Fair point. But look, do you have any ski masks at all?"

"No," I sigh. "My mom doesn't like them. She says they remind her of terrorists and bank robbers. I don't think she processed 9-11 properly."

"Well we can't do a secret mission wearing all this pink and glitter," she gestures at my clothes.

I shrug, uncomfortable. I remind myself that I don't have to defend my clothing choices to her.

She rubs her temples like she has a headache.

"So, here's the new plan. Take off your clothes."

"Wait, what?"

"Yeah." She bites her lip. "I'm going to have to shapeshift us. We're gonna be owls."

"Wait, wait, wait," I protest. "How does that even work? And why? Why owls?"

"See this is why I didn't suggest this in the first place, because I knew you'd react this way." She rolls her eyes like I'm a silly little girl afraid of a scary movie, but I think I'm right to be concerned about this. I mean, you can't just drop "we're gonna turn into owls" on a person and expect them to just roll with it, no questions asked.

"It'll be easy, and we'll be done before you know it," she says.

"Can't we just... go as humans?"

"Well, if we could go incognito, yes. But not if we look like we're trying out for the Lisa Frank Pony Parade."

I glare at her. "That was harsh. And mean."

She nods. "Yes, it was. I'm sorry."

"Apology accepted."

"Anyway," Athena continues, "I'm going to change us into owls, we'll fly to Daniel's, go inside, and use our awesome night vision and hunting prowess to find the cockroach."

"How?"

"What?"

"How are we gonna get inside if we're owls? We can't open doors. We can't open windows."

I imagine us floating outside Daniel's window, pecking at the glass, trying to get someone to let us in, which they most definitely will not. They'll probably call animal control, and animal control will come shoot us down with tranquilizer darts.

Athena blinks at me, shocked. "You know I'm a goddess, right? I can handle a closed door, even in owl form."

"Right."

"Ok, so take off your clothes."

"Yeah... about that... why?"

"Because they won't stay on you when you're an owl. Owls don't wear clothes."

That's a good point. I've never thought about that before, but whenever someone transforms into something else in a movie or cartoon, they always somehow keep their clothes on, and when they transform back, they're wearing the exact same thing they were when they were human. It doesn't make any sense. But maybe that's because these are kids' movies and they don't want to show nudity in them.

"Oh. Ok, then."

I start to take off my clothes, but then I stop.

"Wait. Is this gonna hurt?"

Athena wobbles her head side to side, considering.

"No. It's uncomfortable. And weird. But not painful."

Uncomfortable and weird. I guess that's better than painful, but still not something to look forward to.

"Will we be able to talk?"

"Well, no. Owls don't talk."

"And girls don't turn into owls! I don't know this stuff Athena! This is all really crazy!"

Athena nods sympathetically. "I know. I'm sorry. But this is what we have to do."

I'm freaking out now. I don't want to be an owl. What if I get stuck? What if I'm stuck in owl form forever? What kind of life would that be? I don't want to eat rats!

"Ok, I can see that you're spiraling," says Athena, "so I'm going to make this easy."

She holds out a hand and waves it over me. I know what she's doing, and I back away.

"Wait! Not yet!"

But it's too late. My whole body kind of constricts, like I'm being squished into a sausage casing. My feet curl and shrink, and my socks fall off to reveal little clawed bird-feet. I try to scream, but a hoot comes out instead of a normal human voice.

I'm hooting!

This is easily the weirdest thing to ever happen to me.

But my vision is excellent. I can see everything—teeny tiny little things I never noticed before, like how there's a speck of dirt on the ceiling by the door, and there are a few of my blond hairs stuck to the carpet. Oh man, my room is actually kind of dirty. My mom would be so ashamed to see all this dust. I resolve to give it a good cleaning later, when all this is over.

And I see Athena, too. She's already transformed into a large, beautiful barn owl. I hoot again and she comes and gives me a little nip on my neck feathers.

I have neck feathers. That's a sentence I never thought I'd say.

Athena leads the way. She perches on my windowsill and pecks at the glass with her beak. PECK. PECK. PECK.

THAT is her plan for getting out of here? To crack the glass with her beak?

I hoot at her on purpose. She can't break my window! My parents will kill me!

But then the window sort of...melts. It drips down like pancake syrup, leaving a nice open hole for us to fly out of.

Fly! I'm gonna be able to fly.

You know, I wasn't 100% on board with this whole owl thing, but now I'm realizing it was a brilliant plan, a genius plan, and I'm gonna fly!

I spread my wings, trying it out. I note with amusement that my wings are the same blond color as my hair, the same way Athena's feathers match her dark hair. I wonder if Gemma would have bright orange feathers. If so, that would be one cool-looking owl.

I suddenly feel a stab of guilt. I can't believe we're doing this without Gemma. She would absolutely love this. But she couldn't come to the sleepover because her parents are taking her to some diplomatic dinner at the Capitol.

No one is really sure what her parents do for a living, but they travel a lot, and attend important meetings with government officials. And they have guards, like actual guards, armed with machetes. Not guns or pepper spray or batons. Machetes.

I feel like it's best to not ask too many questions about Gemma's parents.

I promise myself that we will invite Gemma on our next flight, for sure.

Athena is already outside, circling in the air. She is majestic, and I get to join her. I spread my wings. I fly.

———

Flying is even better than I thought it would be. Even though it's dark, I can see everything clearly, and better than clearly. When I flap my wings, I lift up higher into the air, and when I straighten them and keep them still, I zoom ahead, gliding. Once I get the hang of it, it's easy, and I feel like I could do it forever.

When we reach Daniel's house, I don't want to come down. Athena lands immediately, ready to get on with it, but she's used to flying. For her, this is just another day. But for me, this is something special, and I don't want it to end. I want this feeling to last as long as possible.

Athena hoots at me from where she's perched on a branch outside one of the upstairs windows. Her eyes somehow manage to convey an urgent look even though they're bird eyes. I ignore her and her urgent look. I'm flying!

I see a little field mouse scurrying through the grass, and my owl instincts take over. I feel an almost uncontrollable urge to swoop down and snatch it up. I can't believe I'm thinking this, but... the field mouse looks tasty. More than tasty. That field mouse looks positively scrumptious.

Athena is tired of waiting for me. She flies up to meet me and pecks me! It hurts! I hoot at her, but she doesn't care. She pecks me again, letting me know that we have to go into

Daniel's house, NOW.

I try to hit her with my wing, but that was a bad idea, be-cause it makes me sink. I regain my balance and fly higher into the air, trying to get away from Athena and her tyranny. She chases.

Then, out of nowhere, Mr. Cronusson is there, standing big and tall, with his arms crossed, all fierce and scary.

Zeus.

I have a sudden memory of the first time I met him. Athena invited me to her house, and it was the first time I'd been there. I'd been super impressed with how huge it was and how clean and fancy everything seemed to be.

And then Athena said we should go into the backyard and play in the gazebo, and Mr. Cronusson was there, with these strange pieces of armor on his hands. "Gauntlets" he called them. They looked like the kind of thing old-timey knights might wear when they did cool knight things, like fighting dragons and riding horses.

"Cool," I'd said, reaching out to touch one of them. I was a little kid; I didn't know any better. "Are you gonna joust?"

A weird shock went through me when my hand touched the metal. It hurt, and sent me flying onto my bottom. Athena came and helped me up, apologizing. But Mr. Cronusson didn't apologize. Mr. Cronusson stood over me, glaring down at me like I was a dirty little hamster.

"Jousting is for squires and servants. Not for kings," he snarled.

I'd been really scared of him then. Scared of his mean voice and terrifying face.

His face looks exactly like that now.

Athena and I notice him at the same time, and we look at each other, not sure what to do. But in the end, the decision is made for us, as we are forcibly lowered down to the earth.

"Well, well, well," says Mr. Cronusson.

I gulp. Athena flaps her wings in agitation.

"Athena, and the Fanny child, I presume." He glares down at us, and I'm truly afraid. "You know Athena, I have very few rules in my house, and one of them is, you must keep your powers secret. Do you know the horrors that could be visited upon us by the government and its entities, should our true natures become known?"

Athena hoots helplessly.

I want to help her, to explain, but I can only hoot.

Mr. Cronusson pulls a piece of paper from the inside pocket of his suit jacket. He unfolds it, and I see the map that

Athena had drawn of Daniel's house, along with some notes she'd scrawled in the margins, and the printouts on cockroaches.

I glare at Athena. How could she be so stupid? She's supposed to be the smart one!

"From this little blueprint, I gathered that you are planning to find the missing boy. From your notes, I gathered that you have somehow managed to turn him into a cockroach, which is very distressing indeed. Of all the idiotic capers I have witnessed in my lifetimes." He shakes his head, disgusted. "I am truly disappointed in you for many reasons, and on many levels. And so, I will issue a just and swift punishment."

I try to fly away, but I'm rooted to the spot. Mr. Cronusson is not letting me move, holding me in place with his god magic. It's horrible. Being an owl was only fun because of the flying. Without the flying, I'm just a tiny, helpless, voiceless bird.

"I understand that you two wish to enter into a pageant, where you will parade around in front of an audience and display your talents, such as they may be."

I actually feel a little glimmer of hope. Is he going to forbid Athena to enter the pageant? I mean, that would be sad.

But not all the way sad.

"Athena, your talent was to be showing your paintings,

was it not? Well, your paintings are to be destroyed. And in addition, you will be prohibited from creating any more art for a period of time sufficient to teach you obedience."

Athena hoots and flaps her wings. I can't tell if she's angry or sad, but I'm guessing it's probably both.

"And you," He turns to me, and I instinctively cower. "You're a little songbird, yes? Well, your singing voice will be taken from you, for a period of time determined by myself."

He can't do that! He can't! It's not possible.

Athena steps in front of me and shakes her owl feathers and hops up and down, which is a strange move for an owl to make, but I understand why she's doing it. She's defending me. Even though I'd just been glad she was going to be banned from the pageant.

I don't deserve a friend like her.

Mr. Cronusson sighs, like he's bored. "Very well, that is all. You will resume your human forms and go back to Fanny's house. And if I catch you meddling with this cockroach-boy, or transforming into any kind of creature again, your punishment will be worse."

He narrows his eyes, and I know he's serious.

"Much worse."

He snaps his fingers and we're human again, just like that. Naked, cold humans.

I squeal and cover myself as best I can with my hands.

Mr. Cronusson rolls his eyes. "Oh for the gods' sakes," he mumbles. And then I look down and see that I'm wearing a white toga, tied with a rope at the waist. Athena is wearing the same thing.

"Go," commands Mr. Cronusson.

And we do. We get up and walk home.

"ABCDEFGHIJKLMNOPQRSTUVWXYZ!" I shout, and I am ecstatic. I can speak! He didn't take my voice away at all. He was just bluffing. I grin at Athena, full of relief.

"You know, I kind of like this outfit," I say, and it's true. It's very comfortable, and I like how it swirls around my ankles. Zeus also gave me some cool sandals made from rope, which are also quite comfortable. Why did people ever stop wearing togas?

"You shouldn't," Athena grumbles.

"Why not?"

"He meant it as an insult. Where we come from, respectable women don't wear togas."

"Really? Well what kind of women wear them then?"

"Just... don't worry about it. It's fine."

"Oh my god, this night was bananas, Athena. We should

do this all the time, seriously. I don't know why you ever go in human form. And I'm glad your dad was all bark and no bite. I would be devastated if I lost my voice, for real."

"He doesn't do idle threats, Fanny," says Athena, tired and defeated.

It's a quiet night, and we are alone on the street. The only sounds are faint cars in the distance, on a busy street far away.

As an experiment, I hum.

It comes out as an irritating screech, as if I were still a bird. Maybe it's just lingering effects from the transformation.

I need to try an actual song. I choose "Life of Ice."

"Inside this life of ice..."

But all that comes out is unpleasant screeching. I panic. I try to sing louder, a different song, but it all comes out the same.

Mr. Cronusson didn't take my speaking voice. Only my singing voice. It's the meanest thing anyone has ever done to me.

I can't help it. I cry. Athena hugs me, and I cry like a baby.

CHAPTER TEN

I fell asleep crying last night, I guess, because when I wake up my face is still wet, and my hair is plastered to my cheek. Lots of times when people wake up, they've forgotten all about what terrible thing happened to them the day before, but I didn't forget. I haven't forgotten for a moment that I can't sing anymore, and might never be able to again.

Athena is already awake and dressed when I get up. She is serious and worried. Her hair is perfect, and her outfit is super cute. How does she look like that already? I feel like a hag with my messy hair and wet face.

"Are you Ok?"

I shrug. I'm not dead, so I guess?

"Good, because we still have to deal with this cockroach situation."

Oh. Right. I'd sort of forgotten all about that. But yes.

We need to solve that problem.

"Yeah," I agree, like it's been on my mind this whole time, "obviously. But your dad said he'd punish us even worse if we keep messing with this. I don't wanna find out what that means."

I imagine Zeus turning me inside out, so I have to wear my intestines like a belt. Or maybe he'll put some kind of curse on me so I can never sleep again, and I go slowly insane from sleep deprivation. It could happen. I saw it in a movie.

Athena nods. "I understand, but a little boy is a scared insect right now, and he very well might get smushed or eaten by a predator. We can't let that happen. Think of his mom."

I don't want to think of his mom, but I can't help it now. Daniel's mom — all sad and alone and afraid. Thanks, Athena.

"But what can we do?" I ask.

"I don't know," sighs Athena, "but we need to figure it out."

"We also need to figure out how to get my singing voice back," I say. "Wait... maybe it's back already."

I open my mouth to sing, but again, only a terrible screeching comes out. I'm so furious and frustrated I throw a pillow at the wall and scream. It would be more satisfying if I had a big room like Athena, so I could get a really good, dramatic throw. But my room is small, and the pillow hits the wall and just sort of slides to the ground, like it's depressed.

Athena watches me with her arms crossed, like a disapproving nun. Sometimes it's cool that she's so grown up, but other times it makes me want to yell. Like when she gives me this look that she has on her face right now.

"You know, there are more important things than this pageant," she says, "and more important things than singing."

I can't believe she's being so insensitive right now.

"Nothing is more important to me!" I shout. "You just don't care about singing because you can't do it!"

"You're right, I'm not a good singer," she says calmly, "but I am a good artist, and those powers were taken away from me. But you don't see me crying and screaming and whining about it."

Whining? She thinks I'm a whiner? Suddenly I'm furious, just furious. I mean, it's her dad's fault that this is happening to me. And her dad would never have done this if she hadn't been careless and left all her plans laying around for him to find. And none of this would be a problem at all if she hadn't lost control of herself and turned a kid into a cockroach in the first place. I was just trying to be a good friend and help her solve her problem, and look what happened!

"Of course you're not complaining, Athena. Perfect Perfect Athena would never do something so awful. Perfect Perfect Athena will probably just brush her perfect hair and do some perfect charity work about it."

Her mouth gapes open in shock, and I'm glad I've shocked her. I'm glad I'm finally saying all these things to her.

"And another thing." I continue, "I'm tired of you always making me look bad. You know, I might not be a wise, beautiful goddess with magic powers, but I'm a decent person. I'm a good friend! I would never try to make you feel bad about yourself. And if you entered a pageant, I wouldn't enter the same pageant, just so I could beat you."

"Is that why you think I entered the pageant?"

Athena's gray eyes are cold, and she's very still. She kind of reminds me of her dad right now, and it's freaking me out, but I keep my cool.

"Yes."

"Then you don't know anything," she says. "I joined the pageant so I could help you."

"Help me? How? By showing off your gorgeous paintings and probably perfect dance moves and expensive evening wear?"

"No. By giving you the confidence to perform in front of an audience."

For a moment that stops me. What is she talking about?

"Think about it, Fanny. Remember in DC, when you sang in front of everybody? Remember the other day, when you couldn't record, but then I gave you a hug, and suddenly you were brave and sang with no problems?"

I shake my head. What she's saying... it can't be true.

But I remember other things, other times. The time I had to give an oral report on Honduras, and I almost vomited from nerves, but Athena gave me a "pep talk" and then I went up in front of the class and gave a flawless report.

And then there was the time when I had to get an award for math at the school assembly, and I couldn't walk to the front of the gym to accept the trophy... at least, not until Athena put her arm around me and whispered in my ear, telling me to go up and get it.

I don't know what to say. I don't know how to feel about this.

"So... this whole time, you've been, what? Doing magic on me to make me confident?"

She shrugs. "I'm a goddess. It's one of my powers."

And just like that, I'm angry again.

"Oh, are you a goddess with many powers Athena? Are

you? Because it's only come up five or six hundred times in the past two days. Can you talk about anything else? Seriously?"

Athena's eyes are mean and watery, and I don't know whether she wants to cry or hit me. Maybe it's both.

"If that's how you feel, Fanny, then I won't help you anymore. Ok? You can figure out how to perform on your own. And good luck with that."

"Thank you," I snap.

Athena looks at me sadly for a moment, and then she leaves, walking right out the door.

I don't follow her. I don't even want to see her face right now.

CHAPTER ELEVEN

Gemma and I are taking a stained-glass making class our moms signed us up for. The class is held in the community rec center, which is large, and gray, and has a funny mildew smell to it. I actually came here for preschool, but I don't remember too much about it. They have a lot of programs for old people, like "how to write your memoirs" and "watercolor painting for mature adults" and "movie Mondays." And now, apparently, stained-glass making for kids.

I have no idea why moms sign kids up for weird classes like this. Like, who needs to know how to make stained glass? I'm not some medieval monk, working in a church. I think our moms just wanted to go have cocktails at the bar next door, and signing their kids up for something sort-of-educational makes them feel good about that choice. It's silly. Gemma and I don't care if our moms go to a bar. They're adults.

My stained-glass design is simple, just a bunch of triangles, which I'm staining orange, yellow, green and red, to make it fall-festive. Gemma has managed to make a very creepy skull, with an arrow sticking out of it. It's actually pretty impressive. She is adding a bit of red to the arrow, to make it look like it's stained with blood. You'd think it was because Halloween is coming up, but it's not. Gemma just likes bloody skulls and things.

Nobody is paying attention to us, so it's a good time for us to talk about Athena and my singing problem.

"So, this whole time she's been helping you with your confidence?"

"Yeah," I reply. "Without telling me. Like, she's been hypnotizing me with her magic powers. Against my will."

Gemma rolls her eyes. "Don't be so dramatic. 'Against your will.' You make it sound like she was assaulting you. She was helping you."

Gemma doesn't get it. She doesn't have stage fright, and nobody ever hypnotized her without telling her. Unless you count her cousin Barry, who is obsessed with computer engineering and talks about it for hours at a time, until she's so bored she zones out and goes into a weird trance. I've seen it happen at a family dinner at her house. It was creepy.

"You don't get it," I tell her.

"I guess not," she shrugs. "But it doesn't matter if she hypnotizes you anyway if you can't sing. That's your bigger problem."

"I know." I stop working on my orange triangle, because my eyes are full of tears, and I can't see what I'm doing. "I don't know what to do."

"Maybe you could talk to Athena's dad. Say you're sorry, and ask him to give you your voice back."

I think about this. The idea of talking to Mr. Cronusson, asking him for forgiveness, begging... it freaks me out and makes me uncomfortable. I think of him glaring down at me with his black, disapproving eyes, like I'm a maggot, or a nasty cockroach.

Right. That reminds me.

"Gemma, did you do any research on cockroaches? I know you've been busy with your parents' schedule and all..."

Gemma goes quiet.

"It's just, we didn't actually find Daniel," I continue. "Do you have any ideas?"

"I'm sorry," she says, "I just didn't have time, I guess."

I'm not mad at her. Like I said, I know she always has fancy dinners to go to and weird events at the governor's house or whatever.

"It's ok. I'm starting to feel really bad though. I mean, pretty soon, everyone will stop looking for him, and they'll just assume he's dead. His poor mom."

I wonder how long he has to be missing before they declare him dead. A year? Seven years? Will they keep looking for him forever, aging up his picture and posting it on bulletin boards with "MISSING CHILD" printed over it, even though he'd be thirty years old by then?

I remember the news segment I saw this morning, where his mom stood in front of the camera, crying. My mom was watching it on the TV, and she looked like she was about to cry, too. Daniel's mom was wearing an ugly sweatshirt, and no make-up, and looked like she hadn't slept in a thousand years.

"Please, if you have my son, Daniel, please let him go. Send him home to me. And..." her voice cracked and her eyes squinted up, "tell him Mommy loves him."

It was really, really sad.

"I think we should just forget about the whole Daniel thing," says Gemma.

"What?"

"I mean it." Gemma dabs at her skull with brisk, haughty strokes. "He was a garbage person, and now he's getting what he deserves. I say, it's karma."

"Gemma, I know he wasn't very nice to you, but he's still a human being. We have to help him if we can."

"No, we don't. And I think you and Athena should drop it. After all, you don't want Zeus to do something even more terrible to you, do you?"

"Well... no."

"Then stop worrying about that cockroach," she snaps.

"I can't believe you're being like this Gemma."

"Why? Am I supposed to be some saint, who turns the other cheek and lets bullies crap all over me? I can't believe YOU'RE being like this, Fanny. Why are you sticking up for that creep?"

"I'm not sticking up for him! But that doesn't mean I want him to get eaten by a hawk or something."

"He's not gonna get eaten by a hawk," Gemma says, like I'm being ridiculous.

"You don't know that."

Gemma takes a deep breath. "Look, you need to let this go, ok? I'm worried about you. I don't want you getting on the wrong side of a vengeful god. Ok?"

"I don't want to be on the wrong side of a vengeful god either. But I also don't want to be responsible for a kid's death.

I mean, could you live with yourself if something happened to him, and you didn't at least try to help?"

Gemma looks up at the ceiling. "You know what, Fanny? I can't with you right now."

And she rolls off, leaving her creepy skull art behind.

CHAPTER TWELVE

Back at home, I sit in my room, feeling sad and angry. I'm fighting with my friends. I can't sing, which is especially bad, since the pageant is coming up, and singing is my only talent. And my best friend, who happens to be a goddess who's better than me at everything, has turned a boy into a cockroach, and if I try to solve THAT problem, the god Zeus will turn me into a goat or something, which will be an even BIGGER problem.

I'm stressed. People always say how kids have nothing to be stressed about because they don't have to pay bills, but I bet those people haven't had to deal with these kinds of problems.

Normally, when I'm stressed out, I like to put on some music and sing along with it, but that won't work in this case.

Or will it?

What is it people always say? If at first you don't succeed, try try again! It's true that I can't sing now, because a terrifying god put a curse on me or whatever, but it's probably just a mind-over-matter thing, right? I just need to keep trying until my voice comes back.

I turn on my computer and search through my music for inspiration. I need to find an easy-to-sing song, something that won't strain my voice too much. I settle on "He Knows They Can't Hold Us Down." It's perfect. Slow, melodious, and not too high-pitched. Anyone can sing it.

My parents aren't back from work yet, so I can sing as loudly as I want. And so I begin.

It does not go well.

Every time I try to sing, it comes out as a terrible squawk-ing noise. No matter how hard I try, it doesn't get any better. I can talk, but I can't sing. It makes no sense. I wonder if I could maybe try rapping, instead. But no. I don't see myself becoming the next big rapper. That's not what I want to do, anyway. I want to sing!

Maybe I need a drink of water to clear my throat. It can't hurt anyway. I keep trying to sing all the way down the stairs, making horrible, horrible sounds as I walk. It would be funny if it weren't for the fact that singing is so important to me.

There is a knock at the door. I'm not supposed to answer

the door when my parents aren't home, but I do it all the time. What if the person knocking is in trouble, running from a murderer, and I ignore the knock, and then that person gets murdered and it's all my fault?

Parents can be shortsighted in this way.

When I open the door, there is a gorgeous, and I mean GORGEOUS guy standing there. He looks like he's about eighteen, and he's tall and muscular, with golden-brown skin and glasses that should look nerdy, but actually look super cute.

"Hello," I smile up at him. I flick my hair back, hoping he notices that it's especially shiny today.

He doesn't look charmed. In fact, he looks grumpy.

"Are you Fanny?"

He knows my name!

"Yes," I reply.

"Good. We need to talk. Is it a bad time?" He looks around the inside of the house, like he's expecting to see something unpleasant.

"No, why?"

"I heard squawking noises. I assumed you were slaughtering a chicken for supper. If you need to finish..."

My chin quivers. He heard my attempts at singing, and he

thought I was strangling a chicken. That's not good. At all.

"Who are you?" I demand, suddenly remembering that this is a stranger standing on my doorstep.

"My name is Atlas. I'm a friend of Athena's."

Of course he's a friend of Athena's. She WOULD have the hottest guy ever as a friend, and never introduce me. I'm even more annoyed with her now.

"Ok. Well, what do you want to talk about?"

"May I come in?"

Well of course he can come in. I wave him inside and gesture for him to sit on the couch.

"Can I get you anything to drink? Milk? Whisky?" I'm glad I thought to offer him whisky to show how grown up I am. I know a man's needs.

He gives me a strange look and says no. "Look, Athena told me everything, and I know you know all about us, so I'm gonna cut to the chase."

"Wait, 'us'? You mean, you're a god too?"

Seriously, is everyone a god except me?

He nods. "Like I said. I'm Atlas."

"And that's how you know Athena?"

He nods again. "She helped me out once, a long time

ago. Her dad, Zeus... he has a bit of a temper, and he gave me a terrible punishment. Sort of like what he's done to you, but much worse. Athena did what she could to help me, and I'm forever grateful to her."

"What did she do?"

I'm totally fascinated for reasons that have nothing to do with his beautiful eyes.

"Zeus made me hold up the heavens, which were quite heavy, as you can imagine. Athena and my friend Hercules gave me a break. Of course, Hercules then tricked me into taking up the burden again, but still. Athena meant well."

"I'm sorry, I'm confused. What do you mean, you held up the heavens?"

He blinks at me. "I mean just that. I held them up. On my shoulders."

"But that doesn't make sense. The heavens aren't a physical thing you can hold up. The atmosphere is made of particles. It's not... what are you talking about?" I'm starting to think this guy is crazy. I wish I had a phone, in case I need to call the police to have him removed. This is another way parents can be short-sighted. They never think about insane Greek gods showing up at the house when they say I'm too young for my own phone.

He shakes his head, all annoyed. "Look, this isn't why I came here. I came because we need to talk about Athena."

"What about her?"

I don't want to talk about Athena. I want to talk about art and music, and for Atlas to compliment my hair instead of saying crazy things about holding up the heavens.

"She's very upset. She says you're her best friend, and that you hate her."

"I don't... I don't HATE her. I'm just mad at her."

"Well, she thinks you hate her." His voice is so solemn, it makes me feel guilty, like I'M the one who's in the wrong. "Look, I know that her dad messed up your chances at winning the pageant, and I know that's important to you. Believe me, I know how hard it can be to deal with Zeus. But is this pageant more important than your friendship?"

"No. But she doesn't understand why I'm upset! I get that she's really worried about the cockroach thing, but you know, why is it my problem? I didn't transform the kid! It's not my responsibility to fix this. Why can't she see that?"

"I think she does see that," says Atlas quietly, "but you're her best friend, and she needs your help."

I scoff. "Please. She doesn't need my help. She's a goddess. If anything, I just make things more difficult for her."

"She doesn't see it that way. She loves you. She wants your help, and your friendship."

"And I want to sing in the pageant!"

Atlas shakes his head, like he's disappointed in me. It makes me like him less. Who does he think he is?

"I hope you can work things out. Because I've been friends with Athena for a long time, and I haven't seen her this upset in centuries."

Centuries. Wow. It's weird to think how many best friends she's probably had. I wonder if she has a favorite. I guess I'm probably not her favorite at the moment.

Atlas stands. "I'll go now. I've said my piece. Good luck with the chickens," he gestures with his chin toward the kitchen.

After he leaves the house, I sit on the couch, thinking. At first, I'm just mad, because who is this guy to come meddling in my business, telling me what to do? And why does he have to be so cute while he's lecturing me? It's not fair. Guys who lecture you should only be old and ugly and gross so you can hate them properly.

Then I'm sad, because I can't stand to think of Athena home, upset, and lonely, with no one to talk to except her scary dad, in that gigantic, cold house. Maybe one of the cleaning ladies will be nice to her and bake her cookies. Probably not, though. Athena's not the type of girl who adults bake cookies for. She's always so grown-up and competent, they all just sort of… leave her alone. In a way, it's kind of messed up, because even really mature eleven-year-olds are still eleven-year-olds, and they need cookies and love just like any other kid.

Then I'm frustrated, because I can't do the pageant, and I really really want to do the pageant. I mean, technically, I could wait until next year, but that's a whole year that I have to spend dealing with my stage fright. A whole year I could be practicing in front of audiences and perfecting my instrument. A whole year while other singers my age are getting better and better, and I'm just sitting at home doing nothing with my talent because I'm a coward.

There has to be a way I can perform. There just has to be! I wish I had some other talent, something besides singing.

And then something occurs to me. I DO have another talent. And so does Athena.

I have a great idea, the best idea! I rush up to my room and get on the computer and video call Athena and Gemma. I need to talk to them, and I need them to stop being mad at me.

They answer, and I look at their faces as they pop up on the screen. Gemma is sullen and cranky. Athena is red-eyed and sad. We are not off to a good start.

"Ok, girls. First of all, I owe both of you an apology." I look at Athena. "I know you were just trying to do the right thing about the cockroach, and I'm sorry I was so obsessed with my voice that I couldn't see that. And Gemma," I look at Gemma, "I'm sorry I was being annoying about the cockroach. I know you're just worried about me and Athena, and you don't want to see us get hurt." I look back and forth between my friends. "Can we all forgive each other? Please?"

Athena smiles a little and nods. "Yes."

Gemma nods too. "Ok."

"Awesome," I say. "Because I have a really cool idea. Something we can all do together."

"What is it?" Athena asks.

"I'm so glad you asked. You know the pageant?"

Athena rolls her eyes. "Not this again."

I feel a flicker of annoyance, but I push it aside. Her eye rolling is understandable. "Hear me out. I was thinking we could all do a talent together."

"But I'm not in the pageant," says Gemma, logically.

"No, but you can still be part of our talent," I say. "In fact, we need you."

"But Fanny, you can't sing, and all my paintings are destroyed. I tried to make another one and it looked..." she breaks off, her voice cracking, "it looked like finger painting."

"That's what I'm saying. We need a new talent. I was thinking, we could do math."

Athena frowns. "Math? But how do you perform math? We can't just sit on stage and do problems from our math books."

"No, we can't," I say, getting excited, "but we can make a performance out of it. And that's where you come in, Gemma." I look at Gemma, who looks skeptical. "You'll be our assistant."

"I don't understand," says Gemma.

"Ok, picture this," I say, gesturing with wide hands. "Athena, you and I will be the mathematicians. Gemma, you'll be the question-asker. You'll roll up to people in the audience and ask for random numbers, so the audience knows we're not cheating. You'll give us math problems using those numbers, and we'll solve them onstage, in our heads."

"I don't know," says Athena. "That sounds... I mean, are we allowed to do our talent together?"

"We aren't supposed to be allowed in the pageant without taking our clothes off and parading around in swimsuits, but look how that turned out."

Athena grins. Gemma is grinning too. I feel warm and cuddly inside, now that my friends are happy again. And I feel more forgiving, too. It's easier to forgive people when they aren't actively hating you.

Then Gemma frowns. "But. I don't get it. How can you perform together if you're competing against each other?"

I look straight at Athena, meeting her eyes. "I don't want to compete with you, Athena. Not anymore."

Athena gives me a big, radiant smile, and I know I'm doing the right thing.

———————

Later on that night, I think about Atlas, and how he came over, just to talk to me. That was really cool of him. The more I think about it, the more I realize what a great friend he is—so noble and kind. And his shoulders are just amazingly sculpted and wide. I know he didn't literally hold up the heavens, because that's impossible, but with those shoulders, it's almost believable.

I decide to do a little reading about Atlas, online. Apparently, he once waged war on Zeus, Athena's dad. That must be awkward when they hang out and Zeus is there. But maybe it's been so long that it doesn't really matter anymore. Like how when I was five, I got really mad at the neighbor, because he drove over my special rock, and I hated him for like, a whole year, but now I don't care at all anymore, because it was so long ago, and it seems like kind of a silly thing to get mad about now.

I learn that Atlas is known for his endurance. Also, for helping Hercules get some golden apples.

I like yellow apples too! We have so much in common. Like being friends with Athena! And… yellow apples. And probably a lot of other stuff, too.

I decide to write Atlas a letter. Not an email. A letter is old-fashioned, and romantic, and more like what an ancient god would be used to, I think. Also, I don't have an email address for him. I don't have a mailing address for him either, but I'm hoping I'll see him again at Athena's house, and I can deliver it in person.

I imagine myself sashaying up to him in my coolest jeans, with a rainbow crop top, my hair all blow-dried and shiny. I'll sashay up to him and smile, and look into his eyes, and he'll be putty in my hands. And then I'll hand him the letter, all casual and flirty. Maybe I'll give him a cute little wink. I'll have to practice my winking though, because I'm actually not a cute winker at all. When I wink it looks like my face is having a weird spasm.

Anyway. Here it goes:

Dear Atlas,

Thank you for talking to me about Athena. You were absolutely right. It was stupid to let a silly fight like that come between us. You're a really good friend, and I admire that.

I don't know if you know this, but Athena and I are really good at math. We are even doing a math performance at the Junior Miss Super Pretty Pageant, which I'm sure you've heard about. If you come, you can be part of it. We'll make sure Gemma comes to you to ask you for a number. It'll be so much fun, and I know Athena would love it if you came. I would too.

I read up about you online. Is it true that you're known for your endurance? That's so cool! I've always thought endurance runners were the best ones. I mean, anyone can run fast for a few seconds, but it takes a really strong person to do it for a long time. You must be so strong, both mentally and physically.

Anyway, I know you must be busy with god stuff, but I really hope you can make it to the pageant. I'm not sure if you have a girlfriend or anything, but just so you know, the auditorium can get pretty crowded, so it's probably best not to bring anyone else.

Sincerely,

Fanny

I reread the letter and decide that it's pretty good. I think I sound very grown up and mature in it, and I think it was a good idea to compliment him on his strength. I've heard that guys like it when you do that. They like to feel big and strong and power-ful. Which he is, because he's a literal god.

He's a literal god, and I just wrote him a letter asking him to come to a beauty pageant to watch me do math.

All at once, I realize how stupid this letter is. I can't give this to Atlas. He'll laugh at me, or worse, he'll feel sorry for me. He'll give me that look that adults give little kids when they're trying to tell a joke, but it's not funny, but the adults have to humor the little kids, so they just sit there and listen, uncomfortably, waiting for it to be over.

I cannot have that.

Mom comes into my room without knocking.

"Mom!" I snap. "Knock first."

Mom rolls her eyes, like I'm being totally ridiculous, but I'm not. I deserve privacy. Besides, she makes me knock before I go into her room, so she should understand my request.

I realize my letter is sitting on my desk, right out in the open, where she can read it. I hurriedly cram it into my backpack, between two books.

"What are you doing?" Mom asks, looking at my backpack suspiciously, like I might be hiding drugs in it or something.

"Nothing," I say. "Just putting my homework away."

She nods, totally buying it.

"I need you to come do the dishes. We're having a guest."

"Really?" I ask, curious. We never have guests on weeknights. "Who?"

Mom tenses, and I notice that her face looks kind of miserable.

"Mrs. Doyle. Daniel's mom."

My heart sinks and thuds like a bowling ball in the bottom of a well.

"Daniel's mom? Why?"

Mom shrugs a little.

"I guess she wants to talk to you. She says you and Daniel were friends."

"No, we weren't," I say before I can stop myself. But seriously, why on earth does Daniel's mom think we were friends?

Mom looks at me, a little disappointed-looking.

"Well, she thinks you were, so you be nice to that woman."

"Of course I will!"

I mean, honestly. Does Mom think I'm a total monster?

"Good. Now come down and do the dishes."

I sigh and get up from my desk. I'm not looking forward to this meeting at all. Maybe I can make the dishes take a long time, so I have an excuse to miss it. Maybe I can "accidentally" cut myself on a broken dish and have to go to the hospital to get stitches, instead to talk to Ms. Doyle.

I realize how messed up it is that I'd rather have a medical emergency than talk to a grieving mother. I need to get it together. I'm sure it won't be that bad. Right? Right.

CHAPTER THIRTEEN

Mrs. Doyle is the saddest person I've ever seen. Her hair hangs in long greasy strips around her head. She isn't wearing any makeup, and her skin is blotchy. Her nose looks like she's been wiping it all day, and the nostrils are red and crusty. She's wearing sweatpants and a shirt that has some cartoon character on it I don't recognize. Weirdest of all, she has some kind of crown on her head that looks like it's made from a wire hanger. It has green and clear plastic jewels glued on to it.

Overall, Mrs. Doyle looks like a crazy person, but I guess that's understandable. Her son is missing. I can only imagine how Mom would look if I went missing. Probably not as bad as Mrs. Doyle, but pretty bad.

I feel so, so sorry for Mrs. Doyle, sitting on our couch, while Mom hands her a cup of coffee in a plain white mug. But mostly I feel guilty. Because I know what happened to her son, and I can't tell her. I mean, I COULD tell her, but there's no way she would believe me, and also I promised Athena I wouldn't tell her secret.

I imagine how it would go.

"Mrs. Doyle, I know exactly what happened to your son. My best friend, Athena is actually an Ancient Greek goddess who has been reincarnated into a human body. Your son was being a total douche-canoe bully, and so Athena turned him into a cockroach. But don't worry, Athena and I will find him and put him back into his human body."

And then my mom would either punish me for lying or take me to a special place for kids who don't know the difference between reality and fantasy. No thank you.

"I'm so sorry you're going through this," Mom says, sitting down next to me on the loveseat. We are both facing Mrs. Doyle, so we can see all her sadness, face to face. I want to look somewhere else, but I can't.

Mrs. Doyle starts crying, sobbing into her coffee.

I look at Mom, hoping she'll tell me what to do, but Mom just sits, stiffly, like she doesn't know how to handle this either. She won't make eye contact with me. So I just keep staring at Mrs. Doyle, waiting for her to finish crying.

She doesn't finish crying. I'm desperate.

"That's a lovely crown," I say, because I can't think of anything else to say.

But it works. Mrs. Doyle looks at me, confused. Then she moves her hands up to her head and removes the crown, looking at it as if she's never seen it before. Then she laughs.

"Oh my God. I didn't know this was still on. I must look like a lunatic."

"No, not at all," Mom lies.

"Daniel made this for me for Mother's Day, four years ago. I was going through some things and I found it, and... I guess I forgot to take it off."

She starts crying again, and I feel my insides clench. This is horrible, just absolutely horrible.

"Is there anything we can do to help?" Mom asks, and I can hear from her tone that she means it. She really wants to help.

Mrs. Doyle nods and takes a deep breath. But when she answers, she looks at me, not Mom.

"Fanny. Daniel always had such nice things to say about you. I know he was the new kid, and he hadn't really made a lot of friends yet, but he said you were really nice to him, and he liked you a lot."

I have no idea what to say to this. Daniel said nice things

about me? I barely know him. We've never hung out. The fact that he talked about me to his mom at all is weird, but the fact that he made it sound like we're friends is... sad. Really, really, sad.

Suddenly, my skin is hot, and I wish I could squirm out of my body. Everything in me wants to run out of this room, and never see Mrs. Doyle again. But that wouldn't be right.

"I was hoping you might know something. Or maybe you saw something. Even if it doesn't seem important, or if it seemed like not a big deal. Is there anything you can tell me?"

"I... I don't think so," I say, slowly.

"Did you ever see a stranger talking to him? Maybe someone hanging around the school?"

"No," I say, confidently, because I did not see that.

"Did he ever mention... I don't know, a place he might want to go, or something dangerous he might want to do?"

"No," I say again, shaking my head. This is one hundred percent true. Daniel never said anything to me at all.

"The last time you saw him, did he seem Ok?"

The last time I saw him, he was a cockroach. So no, he was not Ok. But there's no way I can tell her that.

"Mrs. Doyle, I'm so sorry I can't help, but I really don't know anything."

Mom puts her arm around me, giving me a quick side hug. It makes me feel a little bit better.

Mrs. Doyle nods, biting her lip. She looks so miserable, I want to blurt out the whole story, but then again, it's not like the truth would make her feel better. After all, life is a lot more dangerous for a cockroach than for a human. It would only make her more worried.

"What have the police said?" Mom asks, gently. "Do they have any leads?"

Mrs. Doyle shakes her head. "They're looking. But so far, there's nothing. It's like he just… vanished."

She starts to cry again, and I can't stand it. I hate watching people cry, especially if I have something to do with why they're crying. The guilt makes me want to jump out of my skin.

"Mrs. Doyle, you don't need to worry. I'm sure he'll be fine," I say.

"Honey," Mom starts, but I cut her off.

"No, really. Me and Athena—that's my friend—we're trying really hard to find Daniel."

"Fanny—" Mom starts again, but again, I cut her off. I know it's rude, but I have to get this out.

"No, listen! We're really smart. We're in the math club and

everything. I'm sure if we keep working at it, we'll find him and get him back to you."

Mrs. Doyle looks at me with the strangest look I've ever seen. It's a mix of fatigue and sadness and amusement and anger, all rolled together. But she doesn't express any of that with her words. Instead she just says—

"That's really sweet of you."

Mom pats me on the leg, but it's not a friendly pat. It's a "shut up and stop saying stupid things" pat. It's the same pat she gave me when I was asking Uncle John about his colostomy bag.

In my defense, after his surgery, Uncle John told me I could ask him any questions I wanted. And a colostomy bag is a pretty interesting thing to have. I couldn't help but be curious.

Mrs. Doyle is standing now, getting ready to go. She moves slowly, like she's been digging ditches for a thousand years. Like she's that kind of tired. I guess maybe that's the kind of tired you get when your son is missing.

"I'd better go. I need to be home in case there are any calls, or in case... you know, in case he comes home."

Her chin quivers, and it makes me feel horrible for her.

"Thank you both. And Fanny, if you think of anything, any little thing, no matter how small... please call me."

I nod at her, not able to get any words out of my mouth. I mean, what can I say? Nothing that would make her feel any better, that's for sure.

Mrs. Doyle writes her number down on a post-it note from her purse. She hands me the little yellow paper and I fold it and put it in my pocket, knowing I will probably never use it. But it would be rude to throw it away, right in front of her.

Mom shows Mrs. Doyle to the door, and I sit on the love-seat, staring at my hands. This whole situation just got a lot more intense. Is Mrs. Doyle gonna come here a lot now? I imagine this. I imagine her coming over every day, asking if I've seen or heard from Daniel. I imagine her showing up at my high school graduation, crying because Daniel should be there graduating, too. I imagine her showing up at my wedding, sobbing, so sad, because I got to grow up and get married, while her son remained missing.

We have to find Daniel. And soon.

CHAPTER FOURTEEN

It's very exciting to be the leader for once. It turns out, I'm pretty good at telling people what to do.

"So I was thinking we could all wear matching outfits for the talent portion. Something like this." I take out my phone and show the girls some pictures I found. The girls in the picture are all wearing the same style of dress, but in different colors. Matching, but distinct.

"Oooh," says Athena, appreciating my awesome taste.

"Tres chic," says Gemma.

We're at Fairy Dust Clothing Company, which is a super cool shop where my mom will only take me on special occasions. Fortunately, a pageant totally counts as a special occasion.

It had been hard to convince my mom to come here, especially since she doesn't really like the idea of me entering a pageant anyway. But I think the idea of me entering a pageant in an ugly dress and embarrassing her and myself is worse. All I had to do was show her pictures of what some of the other girls were planning to wear, alongside pictures of the dresses I already have in my closet, and Mom got the message. I need something new.

Except now she's involved, and she has opinions. This is the problem with being eleven. You have to rely on your mom for money, so you have to listen to her input, even if she has terrible, terrible taste in pageant dresses.

"How about something like this?" Mom asks. She's holding up a hideous pale-blue dress with huge bunches of lace on it, and with waaay too many bows. Like, however many bows you're imagining, it's more than that. It looks like something a toddler might wear if she was playing pretty pretty princess. And not a cool toddler, either. A really unfashionable toddler.

I look at Gemma and Athena. They both have wide, terrified eyes.

"Um, mom? Doesn't cousin Helena have a birthday coming up? Why don't you pick out something for her while we're here?"

"You know, I think you're right," she says. "Good thinking." Mom turns and goes to the little kid section, and I breathe a sigh of relief.

"Ok. Let's get looking," I command.

It takes us a while to find the perfect dress, but I find it. It's a fit and flare knee length dress with a boat neck. Best of all, it's covered in math equations, and it comes in different colors. It is absolutely perfect.

"Gemma! Athena! Come look!"

They are properly appreciative of the amazing dress, and we each get one, in a different color. Mine is red, Athena's is yellow, and Gemma's is green. While we try them on in the dressing room, we practice through the walls.

"Ok, twenty times twenty," says Gemma.

"Easy, four hundred," I say.

"Ok, Athena, four hundred times four hundred?"

"One hundred sixty thousand," Athena replies promptly.

"But Gemma, you'll need to make the questions a little more interesting. If you just throw out numbers, it's not much of a show. Make them into interesting word problems. Can you do that?"

"Absolutely," says Gemma.

"Good."

"Hey, Fanny?" Athena sounds hesitant.

"Yeah?"

"Are you sure you're going to be able to do this in front of an audience? You're great at math, but with everyone watching

147

you... and I know you don't want me to help you."

I sigh. "Yeah, I know. But I have to learn how to perform in front of people, for when I get my voice back. If I ever want to be a professional singer, it's kind of important. It's probably even more important than having actual talent."

Which is true. If you can't sing, there are gadgets and computers that can make you sound good. But there's no machine that can make you get out onstage if you have serious stage fright. Well, unless you count Athena as a machine.

"Well, maybe we should practice in front of some people. Not a lot of people, just a few, to get you used to it."

"That's a good idea. And Athena? I'm sorry I got mad at you for using your powers to help me."

"It's ok. I understand why you were annoyed. I shouldn't have done that without your permission."

"How about this?" I ask. "During the pageant, I don't want you to help me. UNLESS I totally freeze and can't talk. Then, you can give me a little nudge. But don't do it unless you absolutely have to."

"Ok," she says, and I can hear in her voice that she's happy.

We all three come out of our dressing rooms and look at ourselves in the mirrors.

"Oh my god, we are the cutest things ever!" I shout.

Gemma turns her head this way and that. The green of her dress sets off her hair, and she looks dazzling.

Athena smooths the dress down and turns to get a look at the back. She smiles and nods into the mirror.

"We're ready," I tell them.

We pay for our dresses, then leave the shop. Mom did get that hideous blue dress for my baby cousin, and I feel like I should send an apology card to the poor kid. I hope it doesn't scar her for life, having to wear something so ugly.

Outside the store, we head toward the minivan, happy and excited, talking about where we should go to eat. Then, all of a sudden, a gigantic white owl swoops down from the sky, grabs my backpack, which I was holding in my hand, and flies off into the sky with it.

For a moment, we're all frozen in shock. My backpack wasn't super full, but still. It was big, for a bird to just grab like that.

"What just happened?" Mom asks.

"Um," I say, looking at Athena, waiting for her to help. Because this totally has something to do with her. It has "goddess stuff" written all over it. But Athena doesn't seem to know what to say either.

149

"Um… I guess an owl just stole Fanny's backpack?"

Mom gapes at Athena.

Gemma stifles a smile, looking sneakily at her feet.

Then, Mom busts out laughing. This breaks the tension, and we all laugh.

"My backpack! What am I gonna do?" I say, giggling.

"We'll have to get you a new one I guess," laughs Mom. "That's the craziest thing I've ever seen. Don't owls usually hunt at night?"

"And they usually don't hunt for backpacks," says Gemma, unhelpfully.

"So weird," says Athena, grinning big.

"So weird," I echo, also grinning big.

"Too bad we didn't get it on video," says Gemma. "That totally would have gone viral."

But I can't help but wonder why that just happened.

"Was there something in your backpack that an owl might want?" Athena asks, looking at me, with big eyes.

"Um, like what? A rat? No!" I answer.

"Nothing else?" She asks, prodding me with her finger.

"No. Just a couple of notebooks and stuff," I say, defensively. What kind of weird things does she think I carry around with me?

She looks at me a little suspiciously, but she lets it drop. I'm glad. Because I don't need Mom focusing on this any more than she already has. We don't need her asking questions about why owls are acting weird around us.

"Speaking of notebooks," says Athena, changing the subject, "How about we eat at the Sketchpad? It's a cool cafe where artists hang out."

Of course Athena knows the cool artist hangouts. But we look up the menu online, and it looks amazing, so we all agree to eat there. For now, I decide not to worry about the backpack-napping.

CHAPTER FIFTEEN

It's the night of the pageant, and I'm nervous and excited. We've been practicing and practicing, and I know that our talent portion will be a success, if I can just keep it together and not lose my cool. My evening wear dress is gorgeous—a long, navy-blue gown with a poofy skirt and millions of sequins. I've got the choreography down for the opening number. I am ready!

Mrs. Harris agreed to let Gemma be our assistant, even though she doesn't want to compete in the pageant as a contestant. She also agreed to let Athena and I do our talent together. Actually, she didn't agree to it at first, but Athena's dad came in and acted all Zeus-like and scared Mrs. Harris into agreement.

Athena's dad is scary, but it's great when he's on your side. It was actually really cool when he came into rehearsals and barked orders at Mrs. Harris, like she was a bad employee who had screwed up a major account.

I wonder if that's how Zeus treats his employees. Actually, I don't even know what he does for a living. Huh.

Anyway, all of us girls are wearing our costumes for the opening dance. To be honest, I don't love the costume. It's a cheerleading costume, which Mrs. Harris decided to pair with cowboy boots for some reason. It doesn't make sense, since the song we're dancing to isn't even a country song. Also, I feel like real cheerleaders need athletic shoes to do all their tricks. But I guess since we're not real cheerleaders, and we aren't doing any fancy tricks, the boots will work alright. I just hope the audience isn't as confused by them as I am.

For the opening number, Athena and I are in the back, where it's hard to see me. I know that Mrs. Harris put us there to punish us for being difficult, but I don't see it as a punishment at all, and I'm glad I don't have to be right out front. We've done the choreography many times, and I can do it in my sleep. I've been doing extra practices at home, whenever I have free time. I'm 80% sure I can get through this without Athena's help.

"Alright girls," says Mrs. Harris, clapping her hands to get our attention. For once, she's not wearing a suit. Instead, she's wearing a sparkling white evening gown, which is actually really pretty. "It's almost showtime. Does anyone have to go tinkle? Get a drink of water? No?"

Go tinkle? Ew. Who says that? Weirdos like Mrs. Harris.

But now that she said it, it's all I can think about. Do I
have to pee? No, I don't.

Wait, maybe I do.

No, I don't.

What if I do, but I don't realize it, and I pee all over
myself onstage? If I pee onstage, I will never live it down. I
will always be "The Girl Who Peed Herself During the Junior
Miss Super Pretty Pageant." I'll have to move to a new town and
change my name. I will definitely not win the pageant. And I will
never sing again.

No, this is just me being nervous. I don't have to pee.

Stupid Mrs. Harris is getting in my head. I wish she
wouldn't say things.

"Great. You girls are gonna do awesome, I just know it!
Break a leg!"

The music starts. The opening notes ring out from the
speakers, and my heart starts thumping like crazy. I might pass out. I
might faint backstage, and then I'll be disqualified, and then I'll never get over my stage fright, and then I'll have to get a job working in
an office where I'll complain about it being Monday every Monday.

But then, my body takes over, doing the moves, exactly like I've practiced. It's like I've done this routine so many times that my brain can just shut off, and so my body moves without my having to think about it. I'm running onstage, in formation, grinning from ear to ear, even though I don't mean it. We prance around in circles. I do my high kicks. I do my hand gestures.

"I need a hero! I'm holding out for a hero till the end of the night! And he's gotta be strong, and he's gotta be fast, and he's gotta be fresh from the fight!"

This song is super catchy and fun, but when you listen to the lyrics, it really is ridiculous, and it makes me want to laugh. I channel my giggles into a broader smile, and my face hurts from all the smiling, but I keep doing it anyway.

Then it happens. I catch sight of a face. It's not a face I recognize. It's just an ordinary guy, sitting in the audience, right up front. He's probably there to see his daughter or his niece. But he leans over and whispers something to someone, and I get all dizzy. I just know he's talking about me. He's probably telling the cool person next to him about that blond girl in the back and how stupid she looks, and now she's ruining the pageant for the other girls.

My head spins. I'm gonna throw up. I stop dancing and put my hands on my knees. I I breathe through it and manage to keep my food in my belly. I will not vomit on stage. I will not vomit, and I will not pee myself. I need to get it together.

Athena grabs my arm and pulls me to my feet. I brush her hand off. I don't want her help! I can do this. I start going through the motions, but I can't smile, and I can't be energetic. I am not holding out for a hero. I'm just holding out to the end of the song.

At last, the song is over. I take a bow with everyone else. I have sweat trickling down my neck, and my hands and armpits feel all clammy. Athena nudges me and gives me a little thumbs up. I try to smile back, but it doesn't work. I totally messed up the opening number.

We leave the stage and wait for the next segment, which is the Question and Answer portion.

The first contestant is Alesha Stacey. She is super nervous. I can tell because she's biting her nails and shifting her weight from foot to foot. I feel bad for her. At least her dress is super cute. It's a shiny yellow-and-green tunic-style dress, belted at the waist to give it shape. It's not a typical pageant dress, and I think she's really brave for wearing it. In a good way.

Mrs. Harris smiles at her. Mr. Garrison and Mr. Pacheco sit on either side of her, also smiling.

There's so much smiling in pageants! I wonder if toothpaste companies ever sponsor them. If not, they totally should. And dental offices should, too.

"Alright Alesha. What is your favorite subject in school?"

Alesha smiles. She's happy with this question. Or else the pageant training has really worked on her, and she's smiling because she just can't help it. "My favorite subject is history. I love to learn about our past, and the history of our great nation. USA!" She cheers.

The audience likes this, and they clap for her. She comes backstage, grinning.

"Whew. That wasn't so bad."

And it wasn't. I feel myself start to relax. Maybe this will be alright. I can talk about my favorite school subject. Math, because I like numbers. I can talk about the Mathmagicians and our trip to Washington DC. I can even tie that into my love of singing, and how I discovered it on a Mathmagicians trip! I bet the audience will like that answer.

The next contestant is Julia Caldwell, who is Mrs. Caldwell's granddaughter.

"Julia," smiles Mrs. Harris. "What do you look for in a friend?"

Julia stands up straight, her face serious, like she's about to give a presidential address. "I look for loyalty, kindness, and virtue. I want friends who will help me to avoid the temptations of peer pressure, and who will help me make good and healthy choices."

Everyone claps.

Athena and I look at each other and roll our eyes. Julia is such a goody-goody. It's annoying. I guess you have to be a goody-goody when your grandma is a teacher at the school you attend.

"Next we have Athena Cronusson."

Athena smiles at me and heads out onstage. Her head is held high, her posture perfectly straight. She oozes confidence.

Mrs. Harris has a sneaky smile on her face. She looks at Athena with one eyebrow raised.

"Alright, Athena. Most people know Jack London as the author of the famous novel, *White Fang*. But in addition, he was an ardent socialist. Discuss his socialist viewpoints, and how those viewpoints might have influenced his writings."

I gape. I look around at the other girls gathered backstage and they're just as shocked as I am. We all love Athena, and we don't like how she's being treated. I look out at her, worried.

But Athena just smirks.

I smile, knowing what that smirk means.

Oooh, this is gonna be good.

"Well, Mrs. Harris. As I'm sure you know, *White Fang* was not Jack London's only novel. He wrote many overtly political works, such as *The Iron Heel*. He gave speeches for The Socialist Labor party, and was a firm supporter of workers' rights."

I grin. I'm loving this, and I can tell the other girls are, too.

"I think his best known short story, "To Build a Fire" is a great example of how his socialism informed his writing. In it, we see illustrated the dangers of traveling alone, when a man ignores the advice of an elder and winds up falling through the ice in freezing cold weather. In my opinion, this is a parable for the dangers of ignoring the wisdom of our ancestral social structures and proceeding without a social safety net. The importance of a social safety net is, of course, the basic foundation upon which socialism rests."

Athena curtsies, and turns and walks offstage.

There is a stunned silence, and then applause breaks out.

Mrs. Harris is furious, but she hides it with a tight, fake smile. However, I can see that her hands are clenched into fists.

When Athena gets backstage, I hug her, and we giggle.

"That was awesome!" I tell her.

"Thanks!"

"Next, we have Fanny Fitzpatrick."

I can't do this. I can't do it. All the joy I felt at Athena's triumph is gone, and all I feel now is pure terror. I don't know anything about Jack London. I hated *White Fang*.

Athena grabs my shoulders. "Fanny. You can do this."

I shake my head.

"Yes, you can. Do you..." she leans to me and whispers. "Do you want help?"

I shake my head again. It's tempting. But I have to do this myself.

Stiff as a board, I walk out onstage. My motions are unnatural, my steps tiny. I'm moving like a reanimated mummy in an old movie, but at least I'm moving.

I'm onstage. I'm onstage.

I look out at the audience, but I can't see them. The lights are bright, which makes the audience very dark. I can't tell who's out there. This helps. If I saw a guy rolling his eyes, or people talking, or some lady snickering, I'd probably puke for real. If I can't see the audience, my brain can tell itself that they might not be there. I take a deep breath.

"Fanny," says Mrs. Harris, grinning. "When Hannibal Barcas attempted to gain control of Iberia, he started the Second Punic War. His failure to capture Rome was a terrible blow, and he was forced to negotiate peace. Tell us how you would have captured

Rome, and what you would have done differently, in his place."

I can't think. I can't even understand the question she's asking. Hannibal? What? I'm too freaked out to answer. For some reason all I can think about is this bizarre artsy movie I watched on late night TV, where there was this cat-girl who invaded a tofu factory and ate way too much tofu and vomited the tofu all over the place. I am that cat. I am going to spray tofu all over the audience. I've bitten off more than I can chew, and this pageant was a terrible idea.

WHY IS THIS IN MY HEAD?

"Fanny?" Mr. Garrison is looking at me with concern. "Are you alright?"

"Yes," I say, not alright.

I have to say something. My mind is blank. I try to focus and all I can think of is the tofu-eating cat-girl. What was the question again?

"Fanny, your time is almost up," says Mrs. Harris. She is enjoying this, and it makes me hate her.

"Um. Hannibal crosses the Alps or else it gets the hose again."

I run offstage. I can hear the laughter behind me. My face is on fire. I can't believe I said that. It didn't even make any sense.

162

It was the worst answer ever. They're probably going to disqualify me for stupidity.

Athena hugs me. "It's ok, Fanny. It's ok. She's a horrible woman, and that wasn't a fair question. Everyone knows that."

Some of the other girls are crowded around me, patting me, telling me it's ok. I appreciate their kindness, but it's not ok. It's not ok at all. I totally failed.

"Next, we have Toya Salas."

Toya walks out onstage. I can tell she's nervous, and I don't blame her, after the last two questions. But she doesn't need to worry. Mrs. Harris doesn't hate her.

The question comes.

"Toya. What do you like to do for fun?"

Toya relaxes, and exhales, her face smiling in a real, genuine way.

I'm furious. What does she like to do for fun? WHAT DOES SHE LIKE TO DO FOR FUN?

Athena looks at me and shakes her head.

"I know," she says. "I know."

———

The rest of the question-and-answer session goes the same way, with every contestant but Athena and I getting softball questions, which they answer perfectly, of course. There isn't any wrong way to answer "What do you want to be when you grow up?" Or "What is your favorite thing to do with your parents?"

There was a wrong way to answer my question, and I definitely answered it wrong. Which means I'm the only one who screwed up the question-and-answer portion.

Evening wear goes much better, because there's not much to it. You put on your dress, you walk onstage, you walk offstage. You don't have to talk or perform. Even I can handle that. Especially because I look super pretty in my dress. It's not nice to brag, but I do. And I've been walking just fine since I was two, so this part is easy.

Next is talent. First, Chardonnay Knox does a tap-dancing routine. Then Sarah-Jayne Dillon does a cheer dance. Then Sharna Whitworth plays her violin. It's all very nice and normal, and I like watching them perform. We've got some talented girls in this town. It's surprising how many of them can dance so well. I never took dancing lessons. Am I the only girl in this town who has no dance training? Oh well.

Then it's our turn. We have our math dresses on, and we look fantastic. But I'm still worried.

Athena comes up to me and looks me in the eyes. "Are you sure you want to do this?"

"Yes," I say, firmly. We didn't do all this work to quit now!

"Ok. I'm going to help you," she says. "After the Q&A... I think you need it."

"I think that's best," I agree, even though the thought makes me feel funny and tight in my chest.

She nods, looking a little relieved.

We step out onto the stage. Gemma is already in the audience, with her own spotlight. She is wearing her green dress, and her hair is coiffed and polished. She has a microphone.

Onstage, there is a microphone set up for each of us. I stand in front of the one on the right, Athena takes the one on the left. Athena speaks.

"Ladies and gentleman, my friend Fanny Fitzpatrick and I are going to perform a series of math feats for your enjoyment. Our friend Gemma is going to assist us. She's going to roll around the audience and take numbers. Then she'll present those numbers to us in the form of a problem, and Fanny and I will take turns solving the problems. Ready? Ok."

Athena smiles. I copy her. I'm glad I can't see the audience, but honestly, I think even if I could, I'd be alright. I'm nervous, but not the paralyzing, terrifying kind of nervous I was earlier. It's a manageable kind of nervous. I take deep breaths through my nostrils. I try to clear my mind, and just think about the numbers.

Gemma rolls up to a middle-aged gentleman in a red t-shirt. The spotlight follows her and shines on the man. He looks amused and friendly. I'm glad. He probably won't choose a hard number, just to be mean.

"Sir, can you give me two numbers? Any numbers."

"Uh. Ok. Two and seventy."

"Great." Gemma thinks for a minute. "Ariel has two bottles of vodka to share with her four friends. That's not enough vodka. She goes to the store and buys seventy more bottles of vodka, and that's the perfect amount. How much vodka did each friend drink?"

I burst out laughing, and so do some people in the audience. Gemma is so weird.

"Um," says Athena. "Each friend drank fourteen and two-fifths of a bottle. Which seems unlikely."

There is more laughter. I feel good. People like our talent!

Gemma rolls up to another person, this time a teenage boy. "You sir. Please give me two numbers. Any numbers."

"Alright. 2,147, and 8,872." His voice is squawky and smug. I swallow. It's my turn.

"The restaurant has 2,147 plates, 8,872 forks, and zero

wheelchair ramps. If 2,000 of the plates are being used by 2,000 customers, how long will it take for those customers to burn the building down?"

Her question makes no sense, but it's definitely entertaining. Basically the whole audience is laughing. I can't see their faces, but I can hear them, and it makes me smile.

I step to the microphone. "Well, that depends," I say. "Do they get to finish their meals first?"

Loud laughter greets me, and I flush with pleasure. I made a little joke! Onstage! And everyone liked it!

Gemma finds a mother this time, holding a tiny baby on her lap, sitting in the front row.

"You ma'am. Can you give me two numbers please?"

Because she's so close, I can see Gemma clearly now. And there's something in her pocket. Right in front of her dress, in the little breast pocket. I didn't think you could actually fit anything in that pocket, it's so tiny. I thought it was just for decoration. But there is definitely something in it. Something small and wiggly and brown. Something with hair.

My eyes widen, and I stumble in shock. I look at Athena, trying to make eye contact, but Athena isn't paying attention to me. Her eyes are on the mom in the audience.

"Athena!" I stage whisper.

Athena frowns at me, like she wants to tell me to shut up, because we're in the middle of a pageant. And I know that, obviously, but this is important.

I point at Gemma. I point at the identical breast pocket on my dress, then point back at Gemma. Athena sees what I'm seeing, and her mouth gapes open. She turns to me and mouths "Daniel!"

"I know!" I mouth back.

Gemma has her numbers now. "Your average horse has twenty pounds of intestines. If you gut the horse, and the intestines fall out—"

Mrs. Harris snatches the microphone away from Gemma. She does not look happy, even though a few people in the audience seem to be enjoying Gemma's horse intestines question. Not many, but a few. Still, Mrs. Harris clearly wants to shut her down.

"That is quite enough of that I think," she says, smiling tightly. "Let's give a hand to our mathematicians."

Gemma glares up at Mrs. Harris, crossing her arms over her chest. Gemma's mom senses danger and comes and puts a hand on her daughter's shoulder, trying to keep her calm. Gemma bats her mom's hand off her shoulder and says something angry, but I can't hear it, since she doesn't have the microphone anymore.

There is a round of polite applause, and Athena and I rush offstage.

"Do you think she's had him the whole time?" I ask Athena.

"Yes, probably," she says. "But how?"

"What is she doing with him?"

I imagine Gemma doing weird things with her cockroach pet, like making him do tricks for peanuts, or making him fight other cockroaches in some kind of sick death battle. I'm guessing she's not reading him bedtime stories and feeding him tiny mugs of hot cocoa.

"I don't know. We need to talk to her." Athena's face is grim and determined, the opposite of her happy-pageant-smile face. It's not as pretty, but it's a heck of a lot cooler.

"Yeah, we do," I say.

The rest of the pageant is interminable. I feel like it's never gonna be over, like we're gonna be stuck backstage watching girls dance for all eternity. I tap my toes and pace around and crack my knuckles and roll my eyes until eventually it is over, and it's time for the winners to be announced.

Mrs. Harris steps onto the stage and takes the microphone. She is composed and pretty, and if I didn't know any better, I'd think she was a nice lady. I wonder if there's some kind of pageant training that teaches mean ladies how to look like nice ladies.

"Our second runner up … Alesha Stacey!"

Alesha goes out onstage and accepts her award. She's wearing a weird sailor-themed dress, all red, white, and blue, and she does a little curtsy, which the audience seems to think is cute. Who curtsies?

"First runner up, Julia Caldwell!"

Julia accepts her award. It's actually pretty surprising that she didn't win first place. I think she deserves it. Her tap dancing was amazing, and I don't usually like tap dancing all that much.

"And the winner of the Junior Miss Super Pretty Pageant, who will take home a year's gym membership, a complimentary manicure, one thousand dollars, and the title of Junior Miss Super Pretty is…Toya Salas!"

Toya whoops and jumps and runs out onstage, where Mrs. Harris puts a tiara on her head. There are flashes of light, as parents and friends take pictures of the winning girls. They all look so, so, happy.

I should feel sad, and I do, a little. But actually… mostly I just feel relieved. I'm glad this is all over.

Also, there's the matter of the cockroach.

CHAPTER SIXTEEN

Athena and I rush out from backstage, and into the theater. We have to find Gemma. That girl has some explaining to do. I look around and I don't see her, which is odd, since she's easy to spot with her wheelchair and bright red hair. I see her mom, standing in a corner by herself, typing on her phone, probably about some kind of important diplomatic business.

I wonder if Gemma's mom knows about the cockroach. I mean, I'm sure she doesn't know that the cockroach is a boy named Daniel, but maybe she's seen the bug, and just thinks Gemma has found a weird new pet. It wouldn't be too out of character.

Athena and I are almost to the door when my parents stop us.

"Fanny!"

Athena and I look at each other. She shrugs. I nod. We're gonna have to talk to my parents. There's no getting around it. It would be weird if they came and watched the pageant and I just, like, disappeared without saying anything to them.

"That was... really something!" says Mom. She's smiling, trying to be nice, but I can see the confusion in her eyes. She isn't sure what she just witnessed. Neither am I, to be honest.

Dad puts his hand on my shoulder in a very fatherly way. "It's ok that you didn't win, honey. There'll be other pageants."

Mom shoots dad a look. Her eyes are wide.

"Or not. This doesn't have to be a thing now," Mom says, tightly.

"Of course, that's completely up to you," says Dad, looking straight at Mom. "We support whatever you want to do. Because that's what parents are for."

"But sometimes parents have to stop a child from going down a creepy, expensive path," says Mom, staring straight at Dad.

They're about to start bickering about pageants again. Normally, I wouldn't like this, but today, I'm grateful, because if they're arguing, I have a perfect excuse to stay away from them, and they'll be too distracted by their fighting to pay me much attention.

"Hey, thanks guys. We have to go find Gemma," I say.

"Oh, we were just talking to her," says Mom, taking her eyes off Dad, to glance at me. "She said she had to run to the pharmacy on the corner." She waves a hand toward the pharmacy, which is across the street. It's one of those mega-chain pharmacies that is open long hours and has a large selection of lollipops, that they hand out to kids at the drive-through. I used to like to go there a lot, when I was little, because of those lollipops.

"Great, thanks!"

I grab Athena and pull her with me, out the door, through the clusters of chatting people. Some of them tell us "congratulations" or "good job" as we pass, and we smile and say thank you and keep on walking. It's weird that people are saying such nice things to me when I screwed up so badly. Even though I made a fool of myself, no one is treating me badly or making fun of me.

Maybe failure isn't the end of the world.

"Well, that didn't go as planned," I say, as we emerge into the outdoors.

Athena giggles. "No. No, it did not."

"Still, it was kinda fun, anyway."

She tilts her head, considering. "Yeah, I guess it was. And most importantly, you actually stood in front of an audience and talked. You didn't sing, but still. That was definitely progress."

I roll my eyes. "No, it wasn't. I wouldn't have been able to do it without your magic hypnosis or whatever."

Athena stops walking and grabs my arm, looking at me in the eyes. "Fanny, I didn't help you."

"What?"

I think back, remembering. We were about to go onstage, and she gave me one of her mini "pep talks" and then we went out onstage and I didn't faint.

"Yes, you did," I say, but I'm not sure. Because when we went onstage, I WAS nervous. I WAS afraid. I just didn't let it control me. The other times, when Athena helped me, I didn't feel any fear at all, just bold confidence.

She smiles and shakes her head. "No, I didn't. That was all you, Fanny."

A grin spreads across my face, because I know she's telling the truth. I might not have won the pageant—in fact, I performed very, very badly in the pageant—but I found a way to get past my stage fright. And that's the most important win I could have.

We cross the street, and there is Gemma. She's coming out of the pharmacy, holding a bag of cheesy puffs. Daniel is poking his furry little head out of her pocket. She pulls a cheesy puff out of the bag and holds it above his tiny bug-head. The roach reaches his little arms for it, and Gemma pulls the treat away, giggling.

"Hey! Gemma!" I shout.

Gemma drops the cheesy puff and gapes at us. She puts her hand over her pocket, trying to hide Daniel, and she plasters a big smile on her face.

She is fooling no one.

"Gemma, we already saw Daniel," says Athena, crossing her arms over her chest. "We know you have him." Her eyes are flinty, and she kind of reminds me of her dad.

Gemma stops smiling. Her shoulders droop, and her eyes won't meet ours. She keeps her hand over her pocket, though, like she's still trying to hide him, which is silly.

"Yeah," she says. "Kind of."

"So, what's going on? How did you get him? Why are you keeping him? You know his mom is worried." I say all of these things at once, then realize I'm not giving her a chance to answer, so I shut up.

Gemma shrugs. She looks embarrassed and sorry, and I feel kind of bad for her, but I still want answers.

"I don't know," she says, and she sounds like a sullen toddler. It makes me cranky with her.

"You don't know?" I ask.

"You have to do better than that," says Athena. "You know, I lost the ability to make art, and Fanny lost her voice trying to get him back. If you've had him this whole time, and didn't tell us, that's not cool."

"I haven't had him the WHOLE time," she says, finally looking at us. "Just... most of the time."

"Then why didn't you say anything?" I ask. "What were you planning to do? Keep him as a pet forever?"

"No," she says. "Just until he learned his lesson."

I nod, realizing what's happening here. "So you've been, like, holding him hostage."

She gives me a small, wicked little grin. "He needed to be punished. I knew if I told you guys I had him, you'd make me give him back, and you'd turn him into a boy again. But he wasn't ready to be turned into a boy. He still had a lot of learning to do." She smiles and pats her pocket, and I'm a little scared of Gemma right now.

"But I am sorry I didn't tell you. You're right. I shouldn't have kept it secret," she says, looking at us each in turn.

"You shouldn't have kept him captive," says Athena. "That's actually the bigger issue."

"No, it's not," says Gemma, waving Athena's criticism away. "He was a mean kid, and he needed to be taught a lesson. I did that. If anything, I've done a great service for humanity."

I frown. "That's... not what you've done here," I say.

"No. Not at all," agrees Athena.

"You're gonna turn him back into a boy now, aren't you?" Gemma grumbles.

"Of course I am," says Athena, exasperated.

"But won't that make your dad angry?"

That's a very good question, but I know it's not the time to worry about it. We have to do the right thing, and fix Daniel. If there are consequences... I guess we'll just have to deal with them.

"Give him here," snaps Athena, holding out her hand.

"Alright. Let me say goodbye."

Gemma reaches into her pocket and pulls Daniel out. I see that he has a little strip of dental floss tied around his neck, keeping him from running or flying away, which explains why he didn't run or fly away. I flinch, worried about what she'll do to him. But she just sets him in her palm, gently. She carefully removes the dental floss from around his neck. He is twitchy, his little legs working overtime, but he seems none the worse for wear. At least Gemma didn't kill him and stuff him, or pull his legs off.

"Daniel, we're gonna turn you back into a boy now. I hope you've learned your lesson." She holds him in the palm of her hand, peering at him closely. "And if you haven't... well... now you know what can happen, don't you?"

"Gemma!" I snap.

She rolls her eyes at me, like I'm being so annoying, and reluctantly hands the roach over to Athena, who holds him carefully. Athena looks around to see if anyone is watching. It's still light outside, and there are lots of cars on this busy street, plus customers going in and out of the pharmacy.

"This is too public," she says. "We need to do this someplace where no one can see. Let's go back to my house."

"But... what about your dad?" I ask, worried. "What if he's there?"

I know what I just said about us needing to do the right thing, even if there are consequences? But that doesn't mean I WANT there to be consequences. I don't want to do this anywhere near Zeus.

"He's not home," Athena says. "He's got a date."

"Are you sure?" I ask. "What if he comes home early because it's a bad date or something?"

Athena chuckles.

"He'll just find another date. Trust me. He won't be home anytime soon."

That Mr. Cronusson has a very active social life.

So we agree to go to Athena's house. Athena carries Daniel

gently in her hand, and we all follow her.

But as we turn the corner, I see a tall, strapping young man with beautiful eyes, and he's smiling at me. He's wearing expensive-looking jeans and a classy gray peacoat. He looks like a model for something fancy like cologne or sports cars.

Atlas.

"Atlas!" I say, too loudly. I make myself take a deep breath and calm my voice.

"Oh, hi Atlas," says Athena, all casually, like she's not talking to the most beautiful guy on the planet. "What are you doing here?"

He frowns and pulls out a crumpled letter. "I got this invitation, from Fanny," he says, holding the letter out. "It was delivered by owl. Pretty cool, Fanny."

He grins at me, and suddenly the backpack stuff makes sense. The letter was in my backpack. The owl must have somehow sensed that there was a letter in it, addressed to a god, and he went ahead and delivered it for me. It would be totally awesome, if it wasn't so totally mortifying. Had he actually been at the pageant? Had he seen me embarrass myself?

Athena nods, grinning, understanding what happened.

"Oh," she says. "I see. That explains the backpack."

"Who are you?" Gemma asks, looking at Atlas with wide eyes.

"Atlas," says Athena. "He's an old friend of mine."

Athena looks at me and does a sneaky little grin.

"Gemma, let's go into the pharmacy. I need you to help me pick out some lipgloss."

"But I thought we were going to your house to—"

But Athena is already pushing Gemma toward the pharmacy. Leaving me alone with Atlas.

"You did a great job," Atlas says to me, politely.

"No I didn't," I respond.

"Yes, you did. I mean, that woman, when she asked you that question about Hannibal of Barca? I was like, Oh no! I was worried you'd give an actual answer and traumatize a room full of small children," he laughed. "But instead you made a joke and defused the situation. I mean, it wasn't a winning answer, but at least you stayed away from all the blood and gore. I thought that was very classy of you."

"Oh," I say, laughing in a weird nervous way that sounds nothing like my normal laugh. "That's totally why I made that joke. Because I didn't want to get too graphic, and scare the children."

He nods at me thoughtfully.

180

"You know, I was there, in the Second Punic War," he says, quietly, looking around in case there are any passerby listening in on our conversation.

"Really?"

"Really. It was a bloody, horrifying massacre. And I'm glad I didn't have to relive it tonight. So, thank you, Fanny, for your sensitivity."

When he smiles down at me, the corners of his eyes crinkle like he really means it. His shoulders are so wide. I want to rest my head on them and snuggle in for all eternity. I want to hear all about the Second Punic War and make him hot cocoa to soothe his PTSD from battle.

He came to watch me in the pageant.

My body starts to move all on its own, trying to throw myself into his arms. My arms slowly rise. My feet inch closer.

I look up into Atlas' face, and see that his expression has changed. Now he looks uncomfortable.

Before I can make a total fool of myself, a hand grabs me and pulls me back.

"Fanny," says Athena, looking at me intensely. "It's time to go."

I look back to Atlas, who looks relieved. I try not to let that hurt my feelings, because I'm actually relieved too. What was I thinking? Was I planning to actually touch a god? A really, really, old god?

"Yeah," I agree. "We should go. Thanks for coming, Atlas," I say, not looking at him.

"Bye Fanny, Athena. And Gemma, right?"

Gemma nods.

"Bye."

And on that note, having been rescued from social humiliation by my best friend, we head to Athena's house, to restore a cockroach to his human form. No big deal.

CHAPTER SEVENTEEN

We arrive at Athena's house, keyed up and ready to solve this cockroach business once and for all. I can't even tell you how relieved I am that we finally have Daniel. But I'm also nervous about what's going to happen next. I'm sure Athena knows what she's doing. But what if she messes up again, and turns him into a mushroom or something? Or worse—a bear. A giant, terrifying bear who wants revenge.

I'm sure that won't happen though.

But it could.

"Alright, let's get everything set up," says Athena.

"What do you need?" I ask. I imagine her making us beat drums while she sacrifices a goat. I do not want to sacrifice a goat. I'm hoping she just needs us to do some chanting, or maybe burn some incense. That might be kind of fun, actually. We'd be like real witches! The nice, fun kind, not the goat-killing kind.

We're in Athena's gigantic museum living room. She carefully removes Daniel and sets him on the ground. She covers him with a blue and white vase, so he can't get away again. We all stand in a circle around Daniel. I wait for Athena to work her magic.

I'm positive this is the first time a cockroach has ever been on this gleaming white floor. I wonder what the housekeeper would say if she saw this. I wonder if Daniel has picked up any diseases or weird cockroach bacteria. I hope not.

"We're going to need some clothes for him," Athena says. "Since he'll be naked when he transforms."

"Right. Good call," I say. "Do you want me to go get some of your dad's clothes?" The idea of going into Mr. Cronusson's room and taking stuff from his closet is terrifying, but also a little exciting. No matter how much he scares me, the man has excellent fashion sense. I would love to see all the fancy designer clothes he has hanging up in what I'm sure is an enormous walk-in closet. I bet it's all Fendi and Gucci and Balenciaga.

My dad gets all his clothes at Target.

"No." Athena shakes her head. "Dad wouldn't like that at all. Besides, his stuff wouldn't fit, anyway."

I deflate a little, but I know she's right. And I guess, even if Mr. Cronusson's clothes did fit Daniel, he would look kind of

184

stupid in grown-man suits and ties. We've done enough to this boy without making him a tragic fashion victim.

Gemma giggles. "Let's put him in your evening gown from the pageant," she suggests.

"Totally," I agree, just kidding.

Athena rolls her eyes at us. "Grow up, you two. I'm getting him a sweatshirt and a pair of shorts."

I shrug at Gemma. She shrugs back.

"Watch him and make sure he doesn't run away," says Athena, as she heads for her bedroom.

After she's gone, I can't help myself. I need to know all the details.

"So, how did you find Daniel?" I ask.

"It was easy," she says. "I just got some roach bait and laid it around outside his house, then I waited for him to come out. Easy-peasy."

Roach bait! Why didn't Athena and I think of that?

"So you captured him. Then what?" I ask.

"Then I took him home, put him in a cardboard box, and didn't let him out. I fed him and gave him water in a bottle cap. I treated him well, considering he was my prisoner."

"Wow," I say. I've never known anyone who kept someone prisoner before. I wonder if it changed her deep inside, like those college kids who participated in that psychological experiment, where they got to put each other in cages, and they basically turned into monsters.

"But he knew why he was there. I made sure of it."

Her face is dark and sinister. I inch away from her a little. I don't ever want to be on Gemma's bad side.

I wonder what ever happened to those college kids, and if they went on to do scary things.

Athena is back, and she has clothes for Daniel draped over her arm. She looks determined and all business.

"Alright. Let's do this," she says. She approaches the vase, and holds her hands over it, like a faith healer on TV.

"Daniel? I'm going to turn you back into a human now. I want you to stay calm, and not scream, ok?"

There is no response from the cockroach, of course. The vase just sits there, being a vase with a bug trapped under it. I wonder if he's trying to talk under there. Do cockroaches even have vocal chords? I don't think they do.

"I'll take that as a yes," Athena mumbles. She closes her eyes. She is concentrating hard, her posture tense. I'm not sure that this is strictly necessary. I mean, she didn't need to close her eyes and concentrate to turn him INTO a cockroach. But I guess she's trying to take her time and do it right, in case she turns him into a moth or something, and we have to do this all over again.

Then, the vase shoots up into the air, and Daniel is there, right in the middle of the living room. Naked. Gemma and I squeal. I don't mean to squeal, but the nudity takes me by surprise, even though I knew it was going to happen. I catch a full glimpse of his butt cheeks and turn around, shielding my eyes. I do not need to see this.

The vase lands on the ground with a loud CRACK, and splits in two. I hope it wasn't some Ancient Greek artifact that can never be replaced. I break bowls and glasses and vases and stuff all the time at home, but they're from Ikea, and no one cares. Zeus will for sure care if we've destroyed some priceless antique. He will care a lot. Especially if he finds out that we broke it doing magic on Daniel.

"Um, here. Put these on," says Athena, handing him the clothes.

There are rustling sounds, and panting. I keep my eyes averted.

"Ok, he's dressed," says Athena, and I turn back around.

Daniel is indeed dressed, and he's pale and breathing

hard. He is obviously terrified, and I don't blame him. The clothes Athena got for him don't fit him properly, because she's smaller than him. The t-shirt is a plain red one, and it rides up over his belly. The shorts are very, very, tight, and he can't get them zipped or buttoned, and they are bunched up in all the wrong places. But at least all of his private parts are covered.

"It's ok," soothes Athena. "You're back to normal now. I want to apologize for turning you into a cockroach. You have to understand, I never meant for that to happen. I just freaked out when you came at me with the bat, and I lost control of myself. It won't happen again."

Daniel looks at Athena like she's crazy. He looks around at all of us with big, frightened eyes.

"Are you ok?" I ask him. Because he doesn't look ok, at all.

"I..." His voice is rusty and creaky, like an old door that hasn't been used in decades. He clears his throat. "I think I'm crazy."

"No, you're not," I tell him.

He looks at Gemma and flinches. "You! It's... oh man. I don't feel so good."

Daniel bends over and puts his hands on his knees.

"We know how you feel," I say. "This is a lot of take in. But it's all better now, right? You can go back home, to your mom."

"My... my mom?" He looks totally shell-shocked. I hope he doesn't faint.

"Yeah, your mom probably misses you for some reason," says Gemma.

"Not helpful, Gemma," I snap.

Daniel looks at Gemma and backs away from her quickly, like he's afraid she's gonna attack him. I really, really hope he's not right. "Gemma. I'm sorry. I'm so sorry I called you that terrible word. I'm sorry!"

Gemma's face softens a little. "Thank you, Daniel. That's all I wanted to hear."

I wonder how she expected to hear that from him when he was a cockroach, and couldn't communicate, but I keep my mouth shut.

Even though Gemma seems to be in a forgiving mod, Daniel is still freaked out, backing away from her without looking where he's going. He backs into a chair, which startles him, and he jumps. He's panting really hard, and I can see his chest heaving up and down. He looks like he's just sprinted a mile.

"Daniel, you need to calm down," I say, genuinely worried about his health. Can eleven-year-olds have heart attacks? Is he going to have a stroke? Did we change him back into a boy, only to have him die in Athena's living room, wearing Athena's too-small clothes? That would be very, very difficult to explain to the police and Mrs. Doyle.

"I don't think I can," he says. "I'm... I'm going crazy. I'm ALREADY crazy."

"Like I said, you're not crazy," I insist. "Do you want a paper bag?"

I think that's what you're supposed to do when someone is hyperventilating. You give them a paper bag and tell them to breath into it. I've seen it in movies. I don't know why it works, or if it will work, but I figure it can't hurt to offer.

Everyone ignores my paper bag suggestion, so I don't find out if it works or not.

Athena walks closer to Daniel, trying to get him to relax. She is using her most grown-up, authoritative voice, the one that works on pretty much everyone, when she's trying to get them to listen to her. "Daniel. Sit down, and I'll explain everything, alright?"

Now he's angry. He clenches his fists and screws his face up. "You! You're the witch who turned me crazy! Or something. I DON'T KNOW WHAT'S HAPPENING!"

"Like I said, I'll explain. Come with me." Athena takes his arm, but he yanks it back.

"Don't touch me!"

"Ok, ok," says Athena, backing away.

Daniel looks at Athena. Then me. Then Gemma.

Then he turns and runs out of the room, into the foyer. We can hear the door slam as he runs out of the house, and, presumably, all the way home.

Athena presses her lips together. "Well, that didn't go as well as it could have."

"Nothing ever does," I sigh.

"Well, at least he's back to normal now, and we don't have to worry about him anymore."

Stomping thuds come from the spiral staircase. I look up, and there is Mr. Cronusson. He's wearing his usual suit, and his hair is slicked back with gel. I guess that's how he does his hair for dates. It's not the best look for him.

I am petrified. Does he know what just happened with Daniel? Is he mad? Is he going to kill us, or worse? Why is he here, instead of on his date?

But, for some strange reason, he's smiling. I don't think I've ever seen him smile before.

"Hello, girls."

"Dad! What are you doing home?"

"I ran into Atlas at DaVinci's. He mentioned that he saw you three heading toward the house, dressed in matching evening wear, behaving strangely. He suggested that I check on you. I abandoned my date to see what was what."

"Atlas," Athena grumbles.

Athena squares her shoulders and looks at her dad with a bravery I admire. "It was Daniel."

"You mean the cockroach boy?"

"Yes."

There is a terrible, loaded silence. I wait, my whole body tensed, waiting for whatever punishment Zeus wants to inflict on us.

And then—

Mr. Cronusson laughs. Confused, I look at Athena, hoping she can clue me in to what is happening right now. But she just shrugs. She doesn't know either.

"And after I forbade you to go after him?"

Zeus shakes his head, grinning widely.

"Well... yes."

"Good gods, girls. That took gumption on your part!"

We look at each other, astonished.

"So... you're not mad?" I ask.

"On the contrary," says Mr. Cronusson. "You see, this

was a test. A test of your mettle and moral fiber. Would you do what was necessary to right the wrongs you had done? Or would you allow the boy to suffer in cockroach form, rather than sacrifice more of the gifts you have been given?"

I hate Mr. Cronusson so much right now. His face is smug, and his voice is booming, like some kind of haughty preacher in an old-timey movie, like he's laying down some serious wisdom on us stupid sinners. But we are not stupid sinners, and he is not a wise preacher. He's just a mean, mean, ancient god, with bad hair.

"Even after I took away your voice, and your art—the things you love most about yourselves—and threatened to take away still more—still you did what had to be done, and turned that ugly cockroach back into an ugly boy. Why girls, I can honestly say I have never been prouder."

And the truth is, he looks proud. He never looks proud of Athena, even though she's basically the perfect daughter. I bet Athena feels pretty good right now, but I don't. I feel upset and confused, like I've been tricked and manipulated. Which, I guess, I have been.

"But... Mr. Cronusson, that's insane!" I blurt, before I can stop myself. "What if we hadn't found him? What if we didn't turn him back? What then? He could have died."

He totally could have died! Doesn't he care? Isn't he supposed to be a responsible adult? Has he no regard for Daniel or his poor mother?

"Oh pish posh," says Mr. Cronusson. "I would not have let such a thing come to pass. Had you failed to return him to his natural form, I would have done so myself, in a few days or weeks. I would have lured him out with cockroach bait and transformed him immediately."

"Cockroach bait!" Athena hits herself on the forehead, having the same "duh" moment I'd just had.

"I know," I mutter to her.

"Alright girls. Your punishment is at an end." He waves his hand over us. I can feel a strange lump in my throat. It feels like I took a bite of food that was too big, and I'm having trouble swallowing it. Then, suddenly, it's gone, and my throat feels normal again.

Is that it? Is my voice back now?

"And on that happy note, I am off. I have another date this evening. You girls behave in my absence."

Mr. Cronusson leaves, and I'm immediately more relaxed. The whole atmosphere changes, like when you put up Christmas decorations, and suddenly your house seems cozy and festive. That's what it's like when Zeus leaves the room. That man is seriously scary.

"Athena? Don't take this the wrong way? But your dad is insane."

"Yes. Yes, he is."

She doesn't look at all offended, which is good. I guess this probably isn't the first time someone's called her dad crazy. I actually feel kind of sorry for her. It can't be easy to have Zeus as your dad. Though I guess he's probably less scary to her, after all these centuries. Still.

"So... can we do art and sing again?"

"There's only one way to find out," says Athena.

She's absolutely right. So I take a deep breath. I think of my voice, coming out strong and powerful, filling the room. I open my mouth...

And music comes out. I sing a silly song that I remember from when I was in kindergarten called "Orville's Orange Orca," because it's the first song that pops into my head. It's a cutesy little kid song, but if you sing it right, it's actually really pretty.

And my singing is pretty. In fact, it's better than pretty. It's beautiful. I can't help but smile as my voice gets louder and more powerful. Athena smiles too, listening to me. I'm so glad to have my voice back. I'll never take it for granted again, as long as I live.

I finish the little tune and do a sloppy, jokey curtsy, while Athena claps. I sang in front of an audience at last, with no help. It's a good feeling.

CHAPTER EIGHTEEN

Daniel told everyone the truth. He told his mom, our teacher, the other kids at school, the police, everybody. He explained over and over again to anyone who asked that he'd been turned into a cockroach and held captive in a little box. He talked about Gemma, and how she would make him do tricks for cheesy-puffs. He said he'd slept in a little cardboard box. He never changed his story, even though no one believed him.

I've gotta say, I'm a little impressed. I mean, if I had this kind of story to tell, and I told it, and no one believed me, I'm not sure I could stand the pressure. I'd probably just give up and say I couldn't remember what happened to me, rather than let everyone think I'm crazy.

Daniel doesn't worry about people thinking he's crazy. He just wants Athena, Gemma and I to be punished. I guess I can see where he's coming from, but it's still annoying. I mean, we turned him back! And he's totally fine now.

Of course, other people don't think he's fine. The cops and his mom and all the adults seem to think that whatever happened to Daniel was so traumatic that he made up this whole cockroach story, rather than deal with the horrible truth, whatever that is.

And that's why Daniel has to go to see the school psychologist three times a week now, instead of going to gym class. I'm jealous. I wish I could go talk in a nice quiet room instead of doing PE. Maybe I should start making up wild stories and see what happens. Anything is better than running laps and doing pushups and squats.

Anyway, Zeus found out that Daniel's been running his mouth, and he is NOT happy. Athena says she's been trying to calm him down, telling him that no one takes Daniel seriously, and that she's sure that pretty soon he'll convince himself that it never really happened, and everything will go back to normal.

I'm not so sure though. I think maybe Daniel is more strong-willed than she's giving him credit for. If he hasn't cracked yet, maybe he never will.

This is why I've decided to have a talk with Daniel, face to face. He probably won't like it, but I think it's gonna be for the best. Someone has to talk some sense into him. Someone has to get him to shut up. It's for his own protection.

———————

When I show up at Daniel's house, his mom answers the door. She is dressed nicely now, and looks much cleaner than she did when she came to my house. There is no sign of the weird headpiece. I figure she looks better now because her son is home and safe. She smiles big when she sees me.

"Fanny! How nice of you to stop by! Daniel's in his room. I'll go get him."

She lets me into the living room, and I sit down on the couch. I'm actually pretty nervous. This is a weird conversation I'm about to have with him. To keep my brain busy, I look around the room, taking it in.

The house isn't as nice as mine. It's a little dingy, and everything is old and kind of stained-looking. The couch I'm sitting on is made of some sort of woven, scratchy material, and it has a striped-brown pattern on it. The coffee table has a few dirty dishes on it, and a wadded-up paper towel. It's not filthy, exactly, but it's not tidy either. I guess they weren't expecting company.

I wonder if this is what Athena and Gemma feel like when they come to my house. The thought makes me uncomfortable.

In the hall, I can hear Mrs. Doyle talking. "Your friend Fanny is here."

There are muffled voices, and then Mrs. Doyle comes into the living room, with Daniel trailing behind him. He doesn't look at me. He keeps his eyes on his shoes.

Mrs. Doyle frowns.

"Daniel, say hi!"

She gives a weird, nervous giggle, and I wonder why she's so freaked out. Then I remember that Daniel has probably been telling her I'm some kind of witch, and she probably thinks he's gonna try to set me on fire or something, but she's trying to be polite and not freak me out.

So this is weird for all of us.

"Hi, Daniel," I say.

He flicks his eyes at me and nods.

"I'm gonna get you some snacks," says Mrs. Doyle. She rushes away, to the kitchen I guess, leaving me and Daniel alone.

I don't know how long she'll be gone, so I have to talk quickly. I keep my voice low and quiet, so she can't hear me.

"Daniel," I say. "I'm not here to hurt you, ok?"

He nods, still not looking at me.

"But you have to stop telling people about what happened. You know Zeus?"

"Zeus? Like the Greek god?"

He looks genuinely puzzled.

"Yes, exactly. He's Athena's dad. And he's like, really overprotective and paranoid. He doesn't like that you keep telling that story about being turned into a cockroach by his daughter."

"You mean he doesn't like that I'm telling the truth?"

"Well… no. He doesn't. He doesn't want anyone to know about them."

"I'm not gonna lie."

"You don't have to lie. Just stop talking about it," I explain. I'm confused why he doesn't get this. "If you don't, Zeus is probably gonna do something bad to you."

He looks frightened, and I can see that I'm getting through to him.

"Like what?"

"I don't know," I said. "But he took away my singing voice, and that was over nothing, basically. And I'm his daughter's best friend. Who knows what he'll do to you? He doesn't even know you, much less like you."

For a moment, he's silent. Then he shakes his head, violently. I can see he's trying not to cry, and I feel terrible. I didn't mean to make him upset; I just wanted to warn him.

"Doctor Matilda was right. You're not a witch. You're just

a regular girl. You and Athena and that.… Gemma. You're just trying to scare me. But it won't work. I have coping strategies now."

He closes his eyes and presses his thumbs and index fingers together. He seems to be doing some kind of deep breathing, or meditation. I know, because I tried it myself once or twice, to help me get over my stage fright. It didn't work for me, and I doubt it will work for Daniel. I need to defuse the situation.

"Well, you're right. I'm not a witch. None of us are."

His eyes pop open and his zen hands clench into fists.

"Then why are you saying these things? Why are you trying to scare me?"

"I'm not, I'm just trying to warn you! Zeus is after you!"

"I don't believe you!"

"Why? Because your doctor says not to?"

"I don't believe her either!"

"Then what do you believe?"

"I DON'T KNOW!"

Mrs. Doyle rushes into the room, with a plate of Oreo cookies. She sees how upset Daniel is and sets down the plate. She rushes to him and pulls him into a hug.

She looks at me over his head.

"I'm sorry, Fanny. Maybe this was too much today."

"I'm sorry too. I should have called first."

Why didn't I call first? That's just basic manners. But of course, I know why I didn't call first. I knew if I waited another second to go to Daniel's, I'd find a reason to put it off. I had to go right away, while I was feeling brave enough.

"It's alright. I'm glad you stopped by. We both are," Ms. Doyle says.

I'm one hundred percent positive that Daniel is not glad I stopped by, but I don't argue with her. I don't want to be rude.

"This year has been a lot for him, with the abduction, and his dad dying."

I feel sick to my stomach. His dad died? I didn't know that. Suddenly, his bad behavior at school makes a lot more sense. It's like my mom always says: "Hurt people hurt people." If my dad died, I'd probably be a jerk, too, for a while. Not as jerky as Daniel was. But jerky.

"I'm gonna go," I say, standing up. "Goodbye, Daniel. I'll see you at school."

Daniel doesn't look at me. His mom gives me a nod and a tight smile.

I show myself out.

CHAPTER NINETEEN

It's been three weeks since all the cockroach stuff, and things are pretty much back to normal. I mean, as normal as they can be when your best friend is a goddess with magic powers, and you have to act like she's not.

We go to school every day like nothing ever happened. It's kind of surreal. Today is especially surreal, because of what's happening right now.

"Menstruation is nothing to be ashamed of, girls."

Mrs. Caldwell is standing in front of the class, trying to look comfortable and confident, but she's not fooling anyone. We can all tell that she hates this, maybe even more than we do. She has the posture of a lady about to face a firing squad. I would feel bad for her, if she wasn't so terrible at this.

You see, she is in charge of teaching the puberty class we all have to sit through right now. This means we have to hear her say the word "menstruation." A lot. Who calls it that anyway? Don't most people just say "having your period?" That's what my mom says. But Mrs. Caldwell is old, like at least sixty, so maybe that's how she learned to say it.

Athena, Gemma and I are all sitting together in the back of the class. We aren't paying very close attention, mostly because we already know all this stuff. I mean, it's the age of the internet. I think it would be pretty hard to find an eleven-year-old girl who didn't know what a period is. Except maybe girls like Dawn Calhoun, whose parents are very religious, and won't even let her wear jeans. Girls like Dawn Calhoun probably don't know about periods.

Dawn Calhoun isn't allowed to take the puberty class. Her parents wrote a note, and she gets to chill in the library with a book, while we all suffer through this presentation. This might be the first and only time I've ever been jealous of Dawn Calhoun.

All the boys are in a separate room, which seems silly to me. I mean, would it be such a bad thing for boys to learn about periods? Maybe if they learn about it now, they won't grow up to be all weird about it, like my dad is. One time? My mom asked my dad to pick her up some tampons from the store, and he came back with pantyliners, and then he laughed and made a big deal about how he doesn't know these things, because he's a man, like it makes him more manly to be ignorant.

Anyway. Back to Mrs. Caldwell.

"Whenever you start to feel ashamed, as sometimes can happen, I want you all to recite this poem to yourselves."

Mrs. Caldwell passes around a stack of papers with a poem on them. Mrs. Caldwell wrote the poem herself. I know this because it says "By Dina Caldwell" at the bottom. There are little pictures of smiling maxi pads all over the page, which is kind of creepy, when you think about it. The paper is pale pink, and the writing is in a darker pink, with lots of fancy curlicues and stuff. I guess this is supposed to make it more appealing and girly and fun. It is not working.

Gemma snickers as she scans the poem. I give her a sly smile and then look away before I bust up laughing.

Mrs. Caldwell reads aloud—

"Every woman gets one,

Every sentence too,

A period's important

For you and you and you."

Here Mrs. Caldwell points around the room, smiling at the girls she points at.

"It means you can have babies

Which is very special indeed,

So always carry a maxi pad

Just in case you bleed."

Mrs. Caldwell snatches a maxi pad from her pocket and holds it up like a trophy, beaming around at us, like she's waiting for us to clap.

No one claps.

I must NOT look at Gemma or Athena. NO. I will keep my eyes on my wooden desk, and admire the grains in it, and NOT look at my friends.

Gemma raises her hand.

NO.

I look at her and shake my head, but she's ignoring me.

"Yes, Gemma?"

Gemma's eyes are all wide and innocent. She holds up her copy of the poem.

"This is a fantastic tool for us. Thank you. But what if I recite this poem to myself and it doesn't work, because the shame is too great?"

I can't help it. I laugh. I make eye contact with Athena,

and she starts laughing too. A few other girls start laughing as well, and this is not good.

"Smartass," mutters one of the girls in the back, but it's in a good way.

Mrs. Caldwell glares at us. Before period class, Mrs. Caldwell gave us a big speech about how this is a serious subject, and we aren't supposed to make jokes and act immature.

"Girls, this is a serious subject, and you're expected to act with more maturity than this."

We try to calm down, but we can't stop. Sometimes the giggles are like that. It stops being about whatever was funny, and just becomes about the giggling, and you can't stop. I both love it and hate it.

Mrs. Caldwell clearly hates it.

"Enough! If you can't take this seriously, you have to go sit in the library."

Gemma manages to stop laughing, and looks at Mrs. Caldwell with big, serious eyes.

"I don't think I have the maturity to learn about this yet."

"Yeah, me neither," I say, gasping for breath.

We all gather our backpacks and rush out of the room. We hear the other girls laughing behind us, while poor Mrs. Caldwell tries to shut them up. I wonder if they'll get sent out of the room too. Maybe everyone will get kicked out of puberty class, and they'll cancel it entirely, and we'll never have to go through this ever again. It's kind of a nice thought.

As soon as we're out of earshot we start laughing again. The hall is empty and our laughter echoes.

"Have you ever heard such an awful poem in your life?" Athena asks.

"No, I haven't. Why did she write that?" I ask.

"I guess she thought it would make us unashamed of our periods?" Gemma says.

"But why would anyone be ashamed of that in the first place? She's so weird," I say.

We head to the library, where our immaturity will be punished with awesome books.

When we enter, I take a deep breath, like I always do. I love the smell of the library. Something about the mixture of polished wood and paper and old furniture makes me feel scholarly and old-fashioned, like I should be wearing a pencil skirt and hat.

I immediately head to the mystery section, which is my usual jam. Gemma goes for R.L. Stein and stuff like that. Athena has her own book in her backpack; something too advanced for the likes of an elementary school library. I'm just about to pick up a nice, fat, juicy book when I see Daniel talking to Gemma. He's wearing his sweatpants, like usual, but his hair looks clean and brushed, like he's made an effort to look nice. Still. He's not allowed to bully Gemma. Not on my watch.

I stomp over toward them, but stop, when I hear his tone. It's not mean or accusing at all. In fact... he sounds kind of friendly.

"I'm making my own spaceship," he says. "It's not working very well though. I mean, it's cool looking. I designed it to look like a cat stuck to another cat. It's really small and sturdy. But it doesn't fly. I mean, it goes in the air, if I throw it. But it just comes right back down."

Gemma is looking at him with a puzzled expression. Then she says, "What are you using for fuel?"

"Fuel?" Daniel asks, like he doesn't know what that word means.

Gemma chuckles. It's not a mean chuckle, either. More like, gently amused.

"That might be your problem," she says. And she says it kindly!

"Oh," he says, shaking his head. "Maybe. Anyway, I didn't come to talk about my spaceship. I came because I have something to say to you."

"Oh?"

She looks super curious. I'm curious too. I creep a little closer, so I can eavesdrop better. I know eavesdropping is rude, but I need to make sure that he's not about to bully her, that this isn't some mean trick.

"I have this doctor now. And well. I know I was really mean to you before. Like, when I called you that word I called you. And I know I was saying some bad things about you, after that. Like, that you kidnapped me and turned me into a cockroach and stuff."

"Daniel—" Gemma looks alarmed now, looking around to see if anyone is listening. No one is. Except me, of course.

"No, I know it was crazy. See, there's this thing called confabulation? Have you heard of it?"

Gemma shakes her head.

"It's basically when something really bad happens to you, and you forget it, sometimes your brain makes up a weird story that's not true. And my brain made up a story about being turned into a cockroach. And I'm really sorry that I said those things about you. I know now that they weren't true."

"Oh. Daniel. I—"

Gemma is at a loss for words, I don't blame her. His face is so honest, so sincere. He really believes that he made the whole thing up. In a way, this is a really good thing. But in another way, I feel really bad for Daniel.

Athena taps me on the shoulder, and I turn around and see that she's standing right behind me. I guess she's been eaves-dropping too.

I shrug at her.

She shrugs back at me.

"Will you tell Athena that I said I'm sorry?" Daniel asks Gemma.

"Um yeah. Sure," she says, with a big fake smile.

He extends his hand for a shake. Gemma shakes it.

"And hey, maybe you can come over and help me with my spaceship sometime. It seems like you know a lot about them."

"Well, I know that a spaceship needs fuel. That's not a lot."

"Still, you know more than me."

"Well, that's true," she says. "Sure. Why not?"

"Thanks," he says, smiling. "Ok, bye!" Then he walks away.

I step out in front of him. He stops and looks at me, and his face is not friendly.

"Daniel," I start.

"No. I'm not talking to you."

He glares at me.

"But… why? I thought we were ok now."

"Me and Gemma and Athena are. But not you."

"Why not me? I didn't do anything to you! I'm the one you should be least mad at!"

He shakes his head. "You came to my house and bullied me. You tried to tell me that Zeus was after me."

"But—"

"You lied. I was crazy, and you tried to make me crazier."

"No, I didn't! That wasn't what I meant to do at all!"

But Daniel isn't listening to me. He just walks away.

I feel angry and awful. Now I'M the bully? I huff, thinking of all that I've tried to do to help that boy, and now he hates me for no reason.

I head over to Gemma, and Athena does the same. We all start talking at once.

"What happened to him?"

"A little therapy and suddenly he's nice?"

"Do we tell him the truth?"

"NO! We don't tell him the truth. Let him live his lie. It's for the best."

"Is it wrong for us to let him think he's crazy?"

"I mean, it seems like this is good for everybody."

"Is it, though?"

After a while, we stop talking and just sit there, thinking. I mean, a Daniel who builds spaceships badly and apologizes for bad behavior and tries to make friends is definitely better than mean, bully Daniel. But it's gonna take some getting used to.

"I think we should leave well enough alone," says Athena.

"Me too," says Gemma.

"But he hates me now," I whine. "He thinks I was trying to bully him when I went over to his house to tell him to shut up about the cockroach stuff. I was just trying to help, and now he thinks I'm some kind of psycho."

"Huh," says Gemma.

"That's not great," says Athena. "But I bet he'll come around."

"But what if he doesn't? What if he tells everyone what I did, and they all think I'm some kind of creep who torments traumatized kids? What if he tries to get revenge?"

"He won't get revenge," says Gemma. "He doesn't know how."

"He might," I say.

"Do you want me to have one of my bodyguards follow you around?"

"YES!"

"Alright, calm down," says Athena. "Let's not get crazy. Maybe we can just try to make things right the old-fashioned way."

"How?" Gemma asks.

"By being nice," Athena says, like it's obvious. Which I guess it kind of is.

I think for a minute about nice things I can do for Daniel, to make him not hate me.

"Should we all go to help him with his spaceship?" I ask. "I mean, even though only Gemma was invited. Maybe we should all go. I think that kid needs some friends. And this will show him that I'm not a monster. I'm a nice person, who helps."

"I think you're right, Fanny," says Athena. "That's a good idea."

Gemma shrugs.

"Sure."

"We'll need some books about aerodynamics," I say.

"And structural engineering," says Athena.

"And how to make our own rocket fuel," says Gemma.

And we split up to find our materials. Because we have a

new project now. And I have a feeling it's gonna be a good one.

CHAPTER TWENTY

On Saturday morning, I wake up to the sound of tapping on my window. I assume it's a tree branch or something, and I groan and roll over to go back to sleep. But the tapping keeps happening, and it's getting louder and faster, and I can't ignore it anymore. Half asleep, I throw my pillow at the window, but I miss, and it knocks my Math Olympiad trophy off my dresser and onto the floor.

I love that trophy, and if it's broken I'll be very upset with myself. It was the first first-place trophy I ever got. I get up and see that it's fine, which is a relief. The little golden girl statue is still there, on top where she belongs, not chipped or anything.

But that tapping is still happening.

I go to the window and see an owl. It's not Athena; it's a pretty black owl, not the kind you see flying around here, and definitely not the kind you see in the morning. And it is frustratedly pecking at the glass. If I don't do something, the window will break.

I see that the owl has something in its claws. It looks like a rolled-up piece of ivory-colored paper. It's tied with a piece of pale blue string.

"Alright, alright," I grumble, opening the window. The owl flies into my room and drops the paper neatly on my desk.

"Is this for me?" I ask, gesturing to the paper. I guess that's kind of a stupid question, because obviously it's for me, but still, I ask, to be polite.

The owl hoots and stares at me.

"Um. Thank you. You can go now." I gesture to the window.

I start to open the paper, grabbing the little blue string, but the owl pecks at my hand.

"OW!"

I drop the paper on my desk. My knuckles are scratched from the owl's sharp, mean beak. I'm not bleeding or anything. But there are definite scratches.

"What was that for?" I demand, mad at the stupid owl.

The owl continues to stare at me, like it expects something. Suddenly, I remember the time my parents left me home with twenty dollars for pizza, and I ordered the pizza, and when it came the delivery guy just stood there, waiting for something, and

I was confused until he said "It's customary to give a tip."

And then the owl's behavior makes sense.

"Um. I guess you don't want money, do you? What do people usually give you for a tip?"

The owl blinks.

"Oh! I know."

I grab my new backpack — I still haven't got my old one back — and root around until I find a little bag of trail mix. I open it and sprinkle it out on the desk. The owl greedily gobbles the snack, while I watch. I hope there's nothing in there that's bad for owls. Can owls eat peanuts? I know some people can't, but I don't know about owls.

The owl doesn't seem to be sick or anything. In fact, it looks energized and happy, and I think that maybe it was just hangry, and that's why it pecked at my hand like that. It flies out into the morning, and I'm left with my paper.

This is a really weird way to wake up in the morning. I hope it happens more often.

I unroll the paper and see that it's an invitation, hand-written in beautiful calligraphy.

Dear Fanny,

Your presence is requested at the home
of Athena Cronusson, this evening at seven P.M.
Formal dress required.

That's it. That's all it says. I guess it must be from Athena.
Is she having a party? She never mentioned it. Huh. Parties at
Athena's house are usually Big Deals, with caterers and decorations and very hip, cool guests. They always require a lot of planning, and Athena talks about them for ages beforehand. I wonder
why this one is different.

Fortunately I still have my pageant dress, so I don't have
to worry about what to wear. My mom will be glad that I'm getting more than one use out of it, since it was kind of expensive.

I get back in bed. The party isn't until 7:00, which means
I can totally sleep in. After all, a girl needs her beauty sleep before
a formal event.

I show up at Athena's promptly at 7:00 PM. I have my
formal dress on, but also a backpack with overnight things in
case this is a sleepover. I wish I had a backpack that went with an
evening gown, but I don't. I'm not sure evening backpacks even
exist, but they should. Maybe someday I'll design a line of fancy

evening backpacks, with sequins and rhinestones. Maybe even with real diamonds and rubies and emeralds. They'll be the prettiest backpacks in the world, and I'll make a fortune. Everyone will want a Fanny Backpack.

I'll have to work on the name.

I knock on the door, and Atlas answers. He is dressed in a tuxedo and looks too gorgeous to be allowed. He is too good for this earth. He looks down at me with those big, dark, kind eyes and I can't speak. I wonder if he would wear a tuxedo to get married. I bet he would. He's a classic gentleman. But I would marry him even in sweatpants, in which he would also look gorgeous.

He's so gorgeous that I forget to be annoyed with him for tattling on us to Mr. Cronusson.

"Fanny! I'm so glad you could make it. Come in."

He ushers me in, and I see that the whole interior has been decorated with flowers. Way, way too many flowers, so many that if I had allergies I would probably die, but I don't have allergies, so I just gawk. There are roses and carnations and marigolds and baby's breath and exotic flowers that I don't even recognize.

"Follow me."

I would follow him into a volcano. But fortunately, he just means into the backyard. He talks as we walk.

"I know the pageant was a bit of a let-down for you. Sometimes things don't go as they planned. And of course, Zeus was up to his old tricks, so you couldn't perform in the way you might have wished."

I look at his face, and see that Atlas looks sort of irritated. I wonder how bad things are between him and Zeus. I mean, all that stuff from the mythology books was thousands of years ago, right? You'd think they'd be able to work past their issues by now. But then again, I'm no goddess. I don't know how these things work.

"Tonight, we will be having a makeup pageant," he continues, smiling down at me. We are at the back door now, and when he opens it, my breath catches. It's absolutely gorgeous. Candles are lit all over the place, which is probably a fire hazard, but I don't care, because it's so lovely.

Gemma is seated, also dressed in formal wear. Her parents are there, looking a bit bored, but elegant as always. I look around for their bodyguards, hoping to get a glimpse of them with their machetes, but I don't see them. I guess they're like ninjas that way. If you see them, they're not doing their job.

Athena is standing in front of an easel, an artist's smock over her pageant dress, to protect it from paint. She grins and waves at me. Her hair is in a shiny ponytail, and she is the relaxed, confident, happy Athena I'm used to.

Zeus sits next to Gemma's parents, looking distracted, messing around on his phone. I guess he's seen his daughter paint enough that he's not impressed anymore. And I don't think he was ever going to be all that interested in my singing performance. Still, at least he's dressed nicely, in a well-tailored gray suit.

Daniel is there, with his mom. They are not dressed in formal wear, but I guess that's ok. They look happy to be here, so I can forgive their lapse of etiquette. My mom sits next to Daniel's mom, and they're chatting like old friends. I wonder if they're talking about me. I hope Mom says nice things about me, to counteract anything bad Daniel's been saying about me.

My dad sees me and smiles. He looks really proud of me, and I try not to let that make me emotional.

Daniel is looking around with big eyes, like he's never seen a place so elegant and fancy. Maybe he hasn't. I remember feeling the same way the first time I came to Athena's house, and I feel a surge of solidarity with him, even though he hates me right now.

There are a few other kids from school, and some adults I don't recognize. Some of them are holding glasses of punch and plates with little snacks on them. I wonder if they all got their invites by owl too. Probably not.

It's not a huge crowd, like it was at the Junior Miss Super Pretty Pageant, but it's still more people than I'm used to singing in front of. Which is zero. And there are no stage lights, so I can see them all. I can see the expressions on each of their faces. I won't be able to pretend they're not here.

Atlas speaks, and it's so loud it sounds like he's using a microphone. I wonder how he manages to project like that. I guess it's his magic god powers.

"Ladies and Gentlemen! Welcome to the Makeup Pageant!"

Everyone claps.

"This will be a special, exclusive performance by two of the most talented young ladies in Athens. Fanny will be performing a solo piece, and Athena will be painting her, live!"

Everyone claps again. My throat tightens. A solo piece? I didn't know about this. Can I do it? I'm not prepared! And Athena's going to paint me while I sing? What if I make weird faces while I sing, and her painting shows me looking all stupid, and I have to act like I like the painting, which will be super realistic and very well done, but will make me look awful? I'll have to hang that painting up in my house probably, and see myself looking like a weirdo, forever.

But I look around and see all these smiling faces. These

are my family and friends. Well, Daniel isn't exactly my friend, but I don't hate him anymore, anyway, now that he's nice. And he will be my friend, soon. These are my people.

I look at Athena, and she gives me a knowing nod. And I realize that she planned this. She wanted it to be a surprise, so I wouldn't spend all day thinking about it and stressing myself out. She wanted me to come here and sing, in front of people, on my own, without her help.

And just like that, I know I can do this. Athena has faith in me. But, more importantly, I have faith in myself.

And so we put on our very own pageant, just me and my best friend, Athena. I stand on stage, in their amphitheater (because of course they have an outdoor amphitheater) and I sing, while Athena paints me.

I sing, not just "Life of Ice" and "I Hope That He Will Try," but EIGHT songs. I give the first concert of my life, while everyone watches and my friend captures the moment on canvas. It's the kind of thing that would have been unthinkable before now. But after all we've been through, and everything I've learned, it's all possible. Not just now, with a small group, but later, in front of more people. It won't be easy, but with practice, and the support of my friends, I can do it.

As I finish the last note of the last song, everyone claps, even Daniel. I bow, and wipe a little tear from my eye. It's the performance I always wanted to give, and I couldn't ask for a better audience.

Athena stands and bows, and we all line up to look at her painting. It's marvelous. She's made me look so pretty, and realistic at the same time. Best of all, she has totally captured the happiness I felt while I was singing, and I can see it shining in my bright, painted eyes.

Athena gathers me and Gemma to a separate corner of the garden, and we go while everyone oohs and aahs over Athena's art.

"Alright, girls," says Athena quietly, grinning at us. "There's one more thing we have to do."

"What?" Gemma asks.

Athena looks at me and raises her eyebrows. Then she looks at Gemma. "Gemma? Have you ever wondered what it would be like to fly?"

Gemma frowns. "Well sure, I guess. Why?"

"Come with us," says Athena. We grin at each other.

And together, we go.

CPSIA information can be obtained
at www.ICGtesting.com
Printed in the USA
BVHW041111151022
649499BV00007B/106